PATIENTS IN PURGATORY

PATIENTS IN PURGATORY

A REVEREND CHRISTIE MYSTERY

WILLIAM T. DELAMAR

OPEN ROAD
INTEGRATED MEDIA
NEW YORK

ISBN: 978-1-5040-8258-7

This edition published in 2023 by Open Road Integrated Media, Inc.
180 Maiden Lane
New York, NY 10038
www.openroadmedia.com

To all those people who have suffered in nursing homes.

PATIENTS IN PURGATORY

CHAPTER ONE

Behind a door marked "Administrator" in a Northeast Philadelphia nursing home, six men met. The man coordinating the meeting was short and heavy-set with a pear-shaped head. "Is our 'administrator' doing as she's been told?"

"She's under control," said a stocky man with a large head and pointed ears. "She'll do as she's told. She knows she better."

"Good. At Rapid Creek, the occupancy has increased to ninety-five percent. Almost all the patients have no relatives we could track. We moved them in from the other homes when they had no visitors for six months. At that point we thought it was safe. The process is paying off. Between our property 'acquisitions' and our 'product' sales, we are doing quite nicely. We had seventy-five night transfers to our surgical suite in just the last three weeks. We have a productive assembly line, so to speak."

"How is Dr. Rosenfeld doing?"

"He has a backlog but he'll catch up. He is quick and constantly meets demands."

"How reliable is he? Will he keep our confidence?"

"He's wealthier than he has ever been and with his medical license being lifted, he has no other place to go."

"Six nursing homes seem to be about the right number, but if another seems ready to go under, we could use another. Additional resources are always welcome."

At The Church of the One Soul, the Reverend Oxford Christie sat behind his desk, working on his next sermon. He could hear the steady hum of traffic behind him and far below on the Schuylkill Expressway. There was a tap on the door and Elmer Weiss peeked in.

"Ox, can I bother you for a few minutes?"

"Of course. What can I do for you?"

"I'm worried sick. I might have messed up the life of my great-niece, my deceased brother's granddaughter. I don't know what to do."

"What's the problem?"

Elmer sat across the desk from Ox. "My great-niece had a stroke a few years ago and can't care for herself. She's a sweet girl, only thirty-two. She has some mental difficulties at times, hallucinations, voices, sees people who aren't there. Other times she's as lucid as you or me." Elmer shifted in the chair. "Anyhow, I think it would do a lot for her morale if you popped in at the nursing home and had a ministerial visit. I would certainly appreciate it. I get over as often as I can, but I'm really too old to drive anymore, and it's all the way in Northeast Philadelphia."

"I'll be glad to, Elmer. I'm never too busy for visiting in hospitals and nursing homes. What makes you think you messed up?"

"I'm not sure I'm right, but it just seems to me there's something strange about the nursing home. I get an uneasy feeling about the place every time I visit. I'd like your opinion, plus it would mean a lot to Rebecca to have a minister visit."

"Maybe you can go with me. In fact, anytime you want to go,

I'll drive you over. We can both visit her. It's tough being alone in a nursing home. Which nursing home is it?"

"Night and Day Nursing Home on the corner of Sharpless and Sharpless."

"Sharpless and Sharpless? Does that street form a cross?"

"No. It's a right angle . . . or maybe a wrong angle."

"I can't take you this afternoon because I have appointments, but what about tomorrow afternoon?"

"At my age, the sooner the better."

"What, exactly, bothers you about the place?"

"The staff or the lack of it, and something furtive about the few you do see. The place is huge, but I'm usually the only visitor there, if the parking lot is any indication. It's hard to put my finger on it, but something's wrong. Sometimes I see absolutely no staff on Rebecca's floor."

"When are the visiting hours?"

"From two to five and from seven to eight."

Ox looked at his calendar. "What if I pick you up at three? I'll be free by then."

Elmer pushed himself up. "Thanks, Ox. I'll come over here."

As Elmer left, Emmett Roberts and Jessie May Fremont looked in. They were in their police uniforms, obviously still on duty.

Jessie May asked, "Can we see you for a few minutes, Reverend Christie?"

"I always have time for my two favorite flatfoots."

"We want to get married and we want you to perform the ceremony," said Emmett.

"I would really be honored. When do you want to tie the knot?"

"The sooner the better," said Emmett. "We've already got our learner's permit."

Jessie May elbowed Emmett. "He means the license."

"You want to make it a week from now so you have time to send out notices?"

"The notices will all be by phone. Most of our friends already know we've decided."

"Ten o'clock in the morning?"

"Great. We'll let everyone know."

Ox grinned. "I guess we'll have a church full of police."

"In full uniform," said Emmett.

At the Night and Day Nursing Home, the administrator, Susan Starky, stood behind the second-floor railing overlooking the lobby. She watched the front entrance. If they came again, everything would have to be perfect. What if they didn't like her performance? The Group was picky. They didn't just fire you. The rearrangement was permanent, and they had the last word.

CHAPTER TWO

On the way home that evening, Ox thought about Elmer. He seemed really upset. What could be so wrong about the nursing home? The Night and Day Nursing Home. He'd never heard of it, but then he knew little about nursing homes other than some had a bad reputation. Maybe it was good news he had never heard of this one. How long had it been around?

When Ox came in the front door, Barbara was sitting on the couch, an open Mother Goose book on her lap. Martha and Billy were sitting on each side of her. He stood in the doorway and listened.

Martha scolded Billy. "You're breathing on the book."

Billy was indignant. "I can breathe on it."

"You're breathing too heavy on it."

"I breathe light."

"Well, I'm bigger than you so I breathe better."

Barbara got up and hugged Ox. "This has been an interesting day at the Christie residence."

"What's happening?"

"Billy has an imaginary friend. His teddy bear can talk. And Martha thinks Billy is childish."

"Well, that's the job of an older sister. Let the little brother know he's a dum-dum. I speak from experience. I had a bigger sister and a teddy bear once."

"A boy bear or a girl bear?"

"A boy bear. My mother said I was too young for a girl bear."

"Well, you just better watch out for bad girl bears."

"I'm happy with the bad bear girl I already have."

As they all walked into the dining room, five-year-old Martha said with disgust, "Billy pooted and blamed his teddy bear."

Ox mumbled to Barbara, "If you don't have a dog, who else would you blame?"

Billy looked indignant. "It was Teddy." Teddy was propped in a chair next to Billy's place.

"Well, it's time to eat now," said Barbara, "so let's not talk about pooting."

Out in the kitchen, Ox asked, "Anything new today?"

"Not much. I pooted and blamed Teddy. Fooled Billy."

"And Martha. Wow. You must be a ventriloquist. You're such a great mother."

"I want our children to be exposed to the real world."

"Well, that's exposure."

"We're having chicken, creamed potatoes, and corn. That alright?"

"If I said it wasn't, would you throw it out?"

"Go sit."

In the dining room, Ox observed his two children. Martha was sitting in her place doing the same but at three-year-old Billy as though he was hopeless. Billy was keeping up a steady stream of conversation with the teddy bear.

"What does your teddy like to eat?"

"Oatmeal," said Billy.

Martha, disgusted, said, "Teddy bears don't eat."

PATIENTS IN PURGATORY

"Do, too."

Barbara came in carrying dishes. She placed a plate in front of Martha, one in front of Billy, and a saucer in front of Teddy.

Martha looked betrayed.

Barbara kissed her on top of her head and whispered in her ear, "Let your little brother pretend."

Martha smiled and looked all-knowingly at Billy and said, "Of course, Teddy likes oatmeal." She didn't say, "You poor dumb little brother."

Barbara placed a platter of chicken in the center of the table. She scooted out to the kitchen and back with the corn and potatoes. "Coffee coming up."

Ox looked at Billy. "Does Teddy like coffee?"

"No," answered Martha before Billy could. "It keeps him awake." Ox winked at Martha.

CHAPTER THREE

At three o'clock the following afternoon, Elmer strolled in. Ox buzzed the church secretary. "Angel, I'll be out of the building for a while. Elmer and I are going over to the Night and Day Nursing home to visit his great-niece. Please lock up when you leave."

In the car, Elmer said, "Has it ever occurred to you that we must be blessed to have a church secretary named Angel?"

"I think she's earned her wings."

"She's a really sweet person. It's a shame she's all alone."

"Well, you're a nice guy, and you're all alone. A number of people in our congregation are alone. Of course, in a real sense, they aren't. You all have each other. We'll just have to keep meeting at the group dinner each month. I have to wonder why a few romances haven't blossomed. You've all been through a lot together. I know there are a lot of strong friendships."

"I suspect we all just continue to miss our own spouses."

"I guess that's a condition of age everywhere. People can go on living. Who knows? Maybe something will click."

"We'll need to go out Roosevelt Boulevard," said Elmer.

"Right," said Ox.

* * *

When they pulled into the parking lot, Ox gazed in astonishment at the stone building. It was old, judging by the style of architecture, but it had been renovated and all the woodwork was painted white. Sculpted images in the form of angels protruded from the walls. It gave a favorable impression to anyone considering placing loved ones there.

"It exudes trust and caring concern."

"Yes, that's what I thought when I first saw it."

Then Ox saw there was also a graveyard off to the side. "Wow. I'd hate to be housed here and have that as a view through my window."

"Fortunately, or unfortunately, not many of the residents can look out of the windows."

The visitor parking lot was a large rectangle across the entire front of the property. Ox guessed the space came with the property, which seemed to stretch out forever, enclosed by a chain link fence as far as he could see. He drove to the other side of the parking area and scanned down the other side of the building out of curiosity.

"We're the only car in the lot," said Elmer.

There was a second building in back and off to one side. It looked like an old brick schoolhouse. All the windows were painted green. "What on earth."

"I thought that was strange, too. Can't see in or out."

There was an enclosed walkway connecting it to the main building.

"Somebody put a lot of money into this place," said Ox. "I wonder if they managed to solicit donations. Do nursing homes make much profit?"

"Well, I selected it for her because it looked successful. I figured someone was doing something right. Probably a dumb reason."

"The main building looks like a hospital."

"Was a hospital. Went belly-up many years ago. It was vacant for a long time. They probably got it cheap."

Ox pulled back over to the center of the lot and parked. They walked into the building. Inside, it was even more impressive. There were large paintings hung around the walls. They each had a medical motif. The reception desk was straight ahead. Ox noticed a long balcony above with a woman looking down on them. She was dishwater blonde. When she saw Ox looking at her, she moved back out of sight.

The receptionist was a truly ugly man, bald with hair growing out of his nose and ears. He was big, and looked like something from a children's picture book. A nameplate on his desk said "Humphrey."

Elmer signed the guest log. "I'm here to see Rebecca Rhine. Room 223." The receptionist looked at Ox. "He's with me."

"He a doctor?"

"No. He's our minister."

"Okay. Go on in."

He pointed with his thumb to the elevator just behind the reception desk, but Elmer was already moving toward it. Ox noticed the dishwater blonde was back.

When they got off the elevator on the second floor, they were hit by a stench—a strong urine smell. The attraction of the lobby wasn't repeated here. There were people in wheelchairs lining the hallway. One was repeating, "I didn't see nothing. I ain't talking. Don't let them take me away. I didn't see nothing."

"I hear that every time I visit. Poor soul."

Elmer led the way and they walked into Rebecca's room.

She struggled into a sitting position when she saw them. For a relatively young woman, she looked wrinkled and sallow. Her eyes were red from crying, forming a contrast to her pale skin. Ox was struck by her bright yellow hair.

"They took my roommate away. I woke up this morning and she was gone. I asked the aide where she was and she said, 'Don't ask me.' She was fine last night. We said good night to each other. Now, she's gone. Just like that. Did she die? Where is she?"

"Now, Rebecca, don't worry. I'm sure she's okay. I'll tell the aide you need to know. Maybe the patient record says where she is. They probably took her for testing or an x-ray, in which case they may have transferred her to a hospital."

"It's getting late. She's been gone all day."

"I want you to meet Reverend Christie. He's my minister and may be dropping in to see you every now and then."

"Can you find out where my roommate is? Her name's Kitty Laker. Please. I know that sometimes I see things that aren't there, but I'm not crazy. I remember someone putting something over my nose and mouth. When I next looked over at Kitty, she wasn't there. I didn't see them take her out."

Rebecca was so upset, she couldn't talk about anything else. Finally, Elmer said, "We'll go check."

Elmer and Ox left for the nursing station. There was no one there. They looked up and down the hall, but saw only the patients in wheelchairs.

"Strange," said Ox.

"Not unusual. I guess these patients don't need much care."

"Still, there should be someone on duty."

The elevator opened and an aide stepped out followed by the dishwater blonde who was talking. "From now on, I want better records kept."

The blonde saw Ox and Elmer and her expression changed quickly from severe to friendly. The aide hung back but her boss approached them. "I'm Susan Starky, the administrator. I'm so happy to see our residents having visitors. It means so much to them." She smiled at Elmer. "I think I've seen you here before."

"Yes," said Elmer. "My great-niece, Rebecca Rhine is in 223. She's upset because her roommate seems to have disappeared. No one will tell her where she is."

"Oh, probably just out getting tests. I'll check as soon as I get to the office."

"I'd appreciate it if you could have an aide let her know. She and her roommate have become good friends."

Miss Starky and the aide moved down the hall without looking at any of the patients sitting in wheelchairs.

Elmer and Ox went back into Rebecca's room.

"The manager's going to have an aide get back to you. She has to check in her office." Ox thought it strange that there was no record kept at the nursing station.

Forty minutes without word. Finally, Ox went back out to the nursing station to ask. It was unmanned. No aide in sight. He went back into Rebecca's room. "Is there a call button?"

Rebecca looked up and pointed to the top of the railing at the head of the bed. There was a button, obviously out of her reach. Ox pushed it. They waited another fifteen minutes. No aide. Ox went back out. No aide. There was no blinking light on what looked like a callboard. He was beginning to have serious misgivings about the place, too. Finally, he spotted the same aide ambling up the hall. When she reached him, he asked, "Are you the only staff manning this unit?"

"On the evening shift, we don't need nobody else."

Ox refrained from saying it wasn't evening yet. "Did Ms. Starky tell you where Rebecca's roommate is?"

"Which one's Rebecca?"

"Miss Rhine. She's in 223.

"Miss Starky didn't tell me nothing."

"What's her phone number?"

"She gone for the day."

Ox went back into Rebecca's room. "No word yet, and the manager's gone for the day. Elmer, you better call her tomorrow. Maybe by then Miss Laker will be back anyhow. Probably taken somewhere for an x-ray or something."

"You probably need to get back. Rebecca, we'll call the manager tomorrow to find out if Miss Laker is back. You'll probably know before we do. I'm sure she's just out having tests. Don't worry."

"I miss her."

With misgivings, Ox and Elmer headed back through the line of wheelchairs for the elevator.

"I didn't see nothing. I ain't talking. Don't let them take me away. I didn't see nothing."

CHAPTER FOUR

Zipping back along Roosevelt Boulevard, Ox said, "Miss Starky seemed a strange person. She seemed . . . I don't know, a bit furtive when she was standing on the balcony, like she was spying, and then went from stern to overly friendly in the patient wing. Then it was like she put us out of her mind."

"I suppose it's a difficult and maybe thankless job. People don't get well in nursing homes. In a hospital, the staff has the pleasure of seeing patients get better."

"Maybe it's difficult managing the aides. They've apparently not been too responsive to Rebecca. I think we should visit at least once a week. Maybe more as the time permits."

"I'd appreciate that," said Elmer. "I see pluses and minuses when I go there. You hear some dreadful things about some nursing homes. It's difficult selecting one and you have to be careful. I made a list of possibilities before placing her. North and South was first. Rapid Creek was second."

"Doesn't the state conduct inspections on nursing homes?"

"Yes, they were actually getting ready for an inspection not long ago when I was visiting, but you still hear awful things."

"They knew when they were going to be inspected?"

"Evidently, that's the system. I wondered about it, too."

"That seems strange," said Ox. "It gives them a chance to cover up any wrongdoing if they are warned ahead of time."

"Well, you have to wonder how good the inspections are with all the problems one hears about."

"Or how good the inspectors themselves are."

"I'll give that woman a call tomorrow morning. Thanks for driving me over."

It was getting dark when Ox dropped Elmer off at his house. He decided not to stop off at the church. Barbara would be getting dinner ready any time now.

That evening, Ox told Barbara about the Night and Day Nursing Home. They always discussed how their day had been.

"There's something about the place that keeps popping back into my mind. The administrator, Susan Starky, seemed strange. I keep wondering if she's hiding something. Are they hiding their flaws at the expense of helpless people? I can't get it out of my mind. Elmer's niece's roommate disappeared and she can't get anyone to tell her where she is. Then there's the huge size of the place. It's unusual."

"Well, it's obvious you need to go back a few times with Elmer to ease your mind."

Ann Cooke, a nurse aide, sat in the lunchroom of Rapid Creek Nursing Home. She ate her lunch, hating every minute she was there. What a crappy place. That administrator, Boyd Silver, who supposedly ran this place, couldn't care less what happened to the patients. It was the only job she had been able to get. It was a crappy world. If she was white, she could have gotten work any number of places. Her mother had named her Jasmine, a black name. She was doomed before she stepped into any employment office. So she changed it to Ann. A name that could go either way. It helped her get into the Personnel Office, but that was it. She had her degree from Philadelphia Community College. A lot of good that did.

People thought just because it was the North, discrimination didn't exist. It did. It was just kept under wraps. In Alabama, they didn't make any bones about it. At least you knew where you stood down there. What the heck, she knew where she stood up here, too. Nowhere. She was at Rapid Creek Nursing Home. She could remember the time she was happy, but the world was full of bigots. Racial bigots, religious bigots, political bigots.

She gathered up her lunch tray and placed it on the table outside the dishwashing room. The stupid jabbering by the men working in there assaulted her senses. In the hallway, she could already smell the odor of urine. She hated this place, and so did the patients. There was not one person working here she could tolerate. How long would it take for them to fire her? She had to conceal her feelings if she wanted to keep getting paid. She lived in one of the trashiest neighborhoods in Southwest Philadelphia. It was all she could afford. She was heavy enough she could defend herself, and being six feet tall gave her an edge. Still, it was no fun walking home at eleven-thirty at night.

Something had to change.

CHAPTER FIVE

Several days later, Ox called Elmer. "Elmer, want to visit Rebecca?"

"Absolutely, but I don't want to bother you. You sure you have time?"

"Yes. I've been concerned about that nursing home."

"I am too. Have been for some time. That's one of the reasons I asked you to go with me. I thought maybe it was just me, but there's something strange about the place. That Miss Starky keeps making excuses. I keep calling and can't get in to her. This time I'm going to go to her office and demand answers. I'm going to tell her Miss Laker has no family to check on her. So I'm going to be her family."

"Okay. We'll swap thoughts on the way. I'll pick you up in ten minutes.

Going out Roosevelt Boulevard, Ox said, "Okay. Let's swap concerns."

"Well, first of all, it's the size of the place, the number of buildings. The upkeep must be enormous . . . strange for a nursing home. There can't be enough revenue to cover the expense. Think of the heating bills alone. Another is all those people sitting in wheelchairs, basically unattended. They appear to be abandoned. The third is Rebecca's roommate. Add to that the administrator . . . something about that woman."

"Yes," said Ox. "All those things. I got the impression that most of those residents suffer from dementia. That makes them more vulnerable to mistreatment."

"On the other hand, are we overreacting?"

"Well, I guess time will tell us something. Let's be close observers of everything there. It's easy to think those poor souls are just waiting to die."

"Yes," said Elmer, "and that reminds me of the graveyard."

Coming into the building, once again, Ox noticed the administrator, Susan Starky, on duty at her usual post. She moved away when she saw Ox looking up.

They made their way to Rebecca's room.

"Uncle Elmer, she hasn't come back. Something's happened to her. I know it."

"Ox, let's go see that administrator. She said someone would let Rebecca know. She's either incompetent or hiding something,"

"Why don't you stay here with Rebecca and let me go talk to her. She may have told someone else who dropped the ball."

"Okay, but I'm getting disgusted. I can move Rebecca to a more responsive place."

"I'll let her know that."

When Ox walked onto the balcony that fronted on the administrator's office, there stood Miss Starky at her usual post. Ox wondered how she got any work done.

Miss Starky looked surprised to see Ox. "Oh, is there anything I can do for you?"

"Yes, Miss Starky. Rebecca Rhine is deeply concerned because her roommate, Kitty Laker, has been taken away and Miss Rhine doesn't know where she is. She keeps asking and no one will answer her."

"Well, let me check. I'll be right back."

She left Ox standing in the hallway as she ducked through a door marked "Administrator." Ox thought it strange she didn't ask him to follow her, but then he thought again he might be overreacting. Maybe he was being too kind. Someone said ministers see everybody as a star. He wanted to be fair, but realistic.

She was back in a matter of seconds. "I'm sorry to say, Miss Laker is in quarantine. She had a fever and things just got worse. Someone should have told Miss Rhine."

"Yes, it would have been nice if someone had let Rebecca Rhine know."

"Yes, it was a lapse on our part not to tell her. People who are infirm tend to worry more."

"I suspect you get a lot of that. Many hospitals have chaplains. Do you have one? Can I talk to him?"

"No. No chaplain. We just do as well as we can."

"Miss Starky, I'm a minister, I'd be glad to fill that role."

"Oh," she said. "I'm not sure . . . I mean I don't think we could afford a chaplain. Money is tight. We, uh, might be able to go that route at a later time. You could check back with me. Oh, I think I hear my phone ringing." She was gone before he could say a word.

Ox stood on the hallway balcony for a few moments. Then he walked over to her door and tapped on it. There was no answer. He tapped again and then walked in. She was just putting the phone down.

"Ms. Starky, I would gladly volunteer to be chaplain at no cost. It would be my pleasure."

"How kind of you. I'll ask the board to see if they approve. They might feel it to be contrary to the rights of privacy for the patients. Thank you so much. I'll let you know. Now I have a problem down in Dietary. I'll talk to you later."

As she disappeared down the hallway, Ox was aware that she hadn't asked how to contact him.

That evening, Starky picked up her phone and dialed a number. "We may have a problem."

CHAPTER SIX

The huge church swallowed up the wedding party and the guests. Emmett wasn't wearing a tuxedo. He was in full dress uniform. So was his best man. There were about fifty police in uniform, including what looked like about a dozen top brass, judging by all the gold braid. Ox recognized Sergeant Oster, Emmett and Jessie May's boss. He looked around at everything as though he expected to see Jimmy Hoffa or the reincarnation of Bonnie and Clyde. He kept looking up at the high vaulted ceiling as though he expected bats to suddenly appear.

Today was a happy occasion. Weddings always were. Jessie May's maid of honor was also police. She, too, was in full uniform as she came up the long aisle carrying red roses. Ox and Emmett stood near the altar waiting.

Emmett was obviously nervous. "You have the ring?" he asked his best man. "Yep. I'm pretty sure, unless I dropped it somewhere near the sewage drain." It took Emmett a moment to realize his friend was pulling his leg.

Larry Pregle, in spite of his age, pounded on the organ as though to show it who was boss.

Jessie May was now coming up the aisle. She too was in dress uniform. She was carrying white lilies. This was a special event for the police department as well as for Emmett and Jessie May.

The ceremony was short, just as Emmett and Jessie May had asked. Ox was impressed by the truly adoring looks the two of them gave each other. That just enhanced their vows.

There were a large number of the members of the congregation attending. Jessie May had been popular with them from the beginning and they had gradually warmed up to Emmett.

Following the reception, Ox and Elmer drove over to the nursing home. Ox had suggested going over in the morning to see if the activity was any different then. They pulled up in front of the building as a trash truck was pulling away. Empty cans lay strewn about as a man in jeans came out to collect them. They watched him move them over to the side of the building.

"Well, that's one thing that's different," laughed Ox. "Well, proves they have trash."

"Must have been a dozen cans."

"Lots of trash."

"Big place."

"Lots of patients."

"Wonder how many patients," said Ox.

He noticed the receptionist standing inside the doorway, watching them.

"It really is strange there are never any other cars parked out here. Aren't there ever any other visitors? Where do the employees park?"

"I've come to expect it. I've never seen any other visitors here. There could be another parking area for the employees. From what I've seen, it wouldn't have to be a large area."

The receptionist came out and walked over to the car. "Visiting hours aren't 'til after two."

"I dropped over to see Ms. Starky," said Ox.

"She's out right now. Try later. Call first." He ambled back to the building. He turned and glared at them.

"I get the impression his job is to keep people away. Guess we'll have to come back in a day or two," said Ox.

"I think I made a mistake bringing Rebecca here."

"That guy's certainly not a walking endorsement."

"For that matter, neither is the boss lady, Starky."

Ox could see Elmer was worried to the point of being sick. He decided he would come back alone later.

Early the next morning, Ox drove back. He pulled over to the far side of the parking lot and got out of the car. Smoke was pouring out of the chimney of the building in back. It had a peculiar odor. He walked around to it, found the entrance, opened the door and walked in. An employee inside, a little man, was visibly upset "You can't be here."

"Why?"

Flustered, he stuttered, "It's . . . it's off limits."

"Why?"

"It's a private area.

"I'm the chaplain. I'm allowed here. I'm allowed everywhere."

"No, no, no. I have my orders."

Ox decided to see how far he could push him. "I'm here to bless the work that takes place in this building."

"Nobody told me."

"Let's start upstairs."

"It . . . it's locked. I don't have the key."

Wide central steps led up from the large front hall. "The steps aren't locked." Ox headed that way.

The little man ran with him saying, "The stairs are off limits."

Ox spotted an elevator off to the left of the stairs and changed course in that direction. "Is the elevator locked?"

"Please don't get me in trouble. They'll fire me if I let anybody in."

Ox stopped. "I'm Oxford Christie." He held out his hand.

"Uh, I'm Link Unger."

"Link, who will fire you if the nursing home chaplain comes in? Would Miss Starky fire you?"

The little man's face became flushed. Even the top of his bald head turned red. "It's her, sure, but it's mainly that big doctor upstairs."

"What's his name? I'll talk to Miss Starky and explain my need to know everything that goes on in my jurisdiction. I don't want you to feel awkward about me being here." Ox looked up the stairs as a man wearing hospital greens strolled across.

"Yes, sir, that's good. If she says it's okay, it's okay." He was so relieved, he almost collapsed.

"That looked like the doctor just walking across up there. What's a doctor doing up there?"

"I don't know. Nobody told me. You need to go now."

"Why?"

"That could be the big doctor, and he's mean as hell."

"Should I bless him?"

"Oh, Lordy. I don't think so."

The elevator doors closed and Ox heard it hum as it answered a call. He decided to wait and see who came off.

"Link, how long have you been working here?"

It was obvious Link had heard the elevator, too. "Not long . . . well, two years. I need the job." He grabbed Ox's elbow and tried to lead him to the entrance. "Talk to Miss Starky. I'll be glad to show you around."

Ox stooped to tie his shoe. Link did a nervous dance trying to steer Ox to the door. Ox put his arm over Link's shoulder. "Link, was this a school building at one time?"

"No, I mean yes. Yes, it was."

"Has the place been remodeled?"

"I don't know. Maybe."

Ox took a few steps toward the entrance and stopped. "Nice marble floors."

"Yes. Yes. Floors."

"Is it hard to heat this building?"

"Good heating system. Big boiler in the basement."

Ox could hear the elevator humming again. "I hear the Columbia boiler is a good one."

"I don't know boilers. I think Miss Starky is in her office now."

Ox looked up at the ceiling. "Kind of a run of the mill ceiling."

"Yes. Yes. Let me know what Miss Starky says."

Link was desperate.

The elevator door opened and out stepped the big man. He looked at Link like he was looking at a stink bug. Then he saw Ox. "Who the hell are you?" He looked at Link. "What's he doing here?"

Ox held out his hand. "I'm Oxford Christie, the nursing home chaplain. And you are?"

"Chaplain, baloney. What the hell do we need with a stupid chaplain? A garbage man would be more helpful. Maybe you could put holy water in the toilets and clean them while you bless them. Link, you get out of here or get him out of here. Your choice."

"Please, Reverend Oxford."

"It's Chaplain Christie. What are you hiding in this building?"

The big man stared at Ox. "What makes you think we're hiding anything?"

"Your paranoid behavior. What's the big secret in this building?"

"I don't believe Starky hired a chaplain."

"She didn't. Chaplains don't charge for their service. It's part of our commitment and outreach. I volunteered. Some of your patients need help. They seem worried to the extreme. That makes me worry."

"Maybe you should worry about yourself."

"See, that's what I'm talking about. What's so secret about what goes on in this building that makes it off limits?"

"He told you it was off limits?"

"Yes."

"Then why are you still here?"

"To understand why it's off limits."

"You don't need to know."

"Is there any reason why I shouldn't know?"

"Yes. It's off limits. Now get out."

"Well, I know when I'm not welcome."

The big man pushed past Ox. "Chaplain. Why don't you do something useful? Be a telemarketer so people can hang up on you." He was out the door.

"He's going to tell Ms. Starky," said Link.

"Don't worry. I'll tell Miss. Starky you threw me out."

"Man, would you really do that for me?"

"For you, Link, yes, I will. I'm sorry you have to work anywhere near that guy."

"She'll eat me alive."

"I'll make a pact with you. Anytime you have a problem with her, I'll intervene."

"Man alive. You're a real friend. Now if only every day was Tuesday."

"Why?"

"Because Tuesdays the big man isn't here."

CHAPTER SEVEN

Ox now knew something was seriously wrong with that nursing home. He worried not only for Rebecca Rhine, but for all the poor souls trapped in the place, waiting to die. Starky seemed a bit like a shark, and the disappearance of Kitty Laker and the obvious fear of some of the patients or residents fed his suspicions. Link and his antics added to his concerns, and so did the big nameless doctor, if he was a doctor.

He would be able to see that building when the big man wasn't there. He had won Link over. He decided to put it out of his mind until Tuesday. Right now, he had to complete his sermon for Sunday. It was already Thursday and he had miles to go.

Try as he might to concentrate on his work, the place kept worming its way back in. Nothing there seemed to tick right. Something there would bear watching. Then he recalled having heard of a local church with a nursing home watch program. Members of the congregation volunteered to visit patients in nursing homes to show the homes the patients weren't without someone on the outside who cared. The idea was that this would prevent abuse and maybe even neglect. As he thought about it, he recalled it was the Unitarian Church located in the

Germantown section of Philadelphia. He pulled out his church directory and found the phone number. He knew the minister, Nathan Gibbs, from the Inter-Denominational Clergy Group. The Unitarians were noted for social outreach. Maybe he could find out how they did it.

On Tuesday afternoon, when Ox and Elmer walked in, Rebecca was sitting on the side of her bed. Her roommate was back, but wasn't talking. She was asleep.

"They brought her back this morning. She said a few things and then closed her eyes."

As if on cue, Kitty Laker groaned, opened her eyes, and an aide walked in, propped her up, and gave her a pill. Miss Laker groaned a little more and then was quiet.

"What did you give her?" asked Ox.

"Her pill," said the aide and she left as quickly as she had come.

"Her pill," said Ox. "Well, I would never have guessed."

In walked the big doctor. "Oh, it's you. Don't you have any place to be?" He drew the curtain around Miss Laker and gave Ox a threatening look.

"Is Miss Laker all right?"

"You don't need to know."

"Actually, I do need to know. Aunt Kitty's the reason I'm here to start with."

The doctor stuck his head out of the curtain. "She's not your aunt. We checked. She has no relatives."

"Why on earth would you do that?"

"Why don't you mind your own business?"

"Well, you see, this is my business. In fact, it's everybody's business how people are treated in nursing homes."

"That's where you're wrong. Stick your nose in my business and I'll have you escorted out of the building." The doctor stepped out from the curtains, stuck his head out of the room and shouted, "Get me a gurney."

Almost immediately, two orderlies pushed in a litter. One orderly looked like the clone of the ugly receptionist in the front. The other was tall, skinny and bald. He looked like a newborn chick.

"Get that patient back to the infirmary. She's got an infection."

Ox and Elmer watched as the orderlies slid Miss Laker off the bed and onto the litter. Her only words were, "Oh, no."

"What kind of infection?" asked Elmer.

"That's her business."

"Is it something catching?"

"Don't worry about it."

"Well, I do worry about it if it's something my great-niece can catch." Elmer turned to Ox. "I think maybe I should move Rebecca to a different nursing home."

"Hardly necessary," said the doctor as they wheeled Kitty Laker out.

Rebecca whispered, "They told her if she talked about it, they would remove her arms and legs and cut out her tongue."

"Are you sure?" asked Elmer. He whispered to Ox, "I hope she's imagining that."

"Goodbye, Kitty," called Rebecca.

CHAPTER EIGHT

The following afternoon, Ox and Elmer went back to the nursing home. "If we are constantly in the place, she's going to get proper care," said Ox.

Elmer was obviously distraught. "I trusted them to take care of her. I should have been more careful."

"It's not your fault. The place looks good. I suspect a lot of people have trusted them. It's more and more obvious the state needs to do something about its inspection process. It's not working."

They pulled into the lot and Ox decided to park on the far side so he could see the building that was off-limits. There was an ambulance parked back there. The driver was standing by it as though waiting for something.

"Let's go see what he's waiting for."

As they approached, the same two orderlies who had wheeled out Miss Laker emerged from the back entrance with a patient on a gurney.

Ox asked the driver, "Where are you taking the patient?"

"To the hospital."

They could tell it was an elderly woman even though she was completely bald. There wasn't a hair on her head.

"What's the problem?"

"Bed sores. Covered with bed sores." The driver looked disgusted. "I'm always picking up patients here and taking them to the hospital for this same reason.

He opened the back door of the ambulance and told the orderlies, "Slide her in here."

"We know," said the skinny one.

"Have you reported them to the Pennsylvania Health Department?" asked Ox.

"I have, but nobody does anything."

"Do you know if the hospital reports them?"

"I know they don't, because they don't want to stop the admissions. They fix them up and ship them back and collect their Medicare or Medicaid fees."

Elmer shook his head. "What kind of world are we living in?" Ox and Elmer walked back around to the front.

Elmer was still shaking his head. "I've let her down."

"Elmer, don't blame yourself. Blame the Health Department for being too lax."

Inside, Miss Starky was already retreating when Ox glanced up. Ox wondered if she was watching out for someone . . . the police. Would she scamper if it was the police? The receptionist just looked at them. On the way up on the elevator, Ox thought of Emmett and Jessie May. When they got back from their honeymoon, he would ask them if they ever received complaints about Night and Day Nursing Home or any other nursing home. He decided not to mention that to Elmer. He was already distraught.

Rebecca was sitting up when they walked in. "Uncle Elmer, they took away another sleeping room roommate."

"I guess that's annoying. Probably needed x-rays or something. In the meantime, relax. We assume she's in good hands."

His look to Ox said he didn't believe it. "How are you? Are they doing everything they need to?"

"I don't need much, but I miss Kitty."

Ox walked over to the window. He could see the graveyard. From the higher vantage point, in addition to the few tombstones there appeared to be some kind of markers spaced out over the plot. The markers were only a few feet apart. Not very large for gravesites. Maybe they were just cremated. It occurred to him that if they were cremated, there could be no autopsy.

Talk about paranoia. He would have to look later, but not with Elmer. He already planned to come over Tuesday, when the 'big doctor' wasn't there to see what was going on in the off-limits building. He would poke around in the graveyard then. This place was getting to be a habit. He would also check with Nathan Gibbs at the Unitarian Church to see about a nursing home watch program.

Driving back, Ox mentioned Nathan Gibbs and the nursing home watch program.

Elmer immediately became interested. "Maybe they have a listing of the better nursing homes."

"I'm sure they could tell us some to avoid if nothing else."

"I wonder if there's a list of the problem-free ones," said Elmer.

"I wonder if there is such a thing as a problem-free nursing home."

Then a thought struck Ox. "What if we placed Rebecca in the mansion Hosanna Lewis left us? The woman left us millions and the mansion. We owe it to her to do something memorable. Volunteers could take turns looking after Rebecca." Immediately, he thought of reasons why it wouldn't work. "Forget it. Someone would have to cook. Someone would have to clean. We would have to have a staff of people. Not to mention the need for nursing care."

"Well, wait a minute," said Elmer. "Why not convert that mansion into our own nursing home. Lord knows we've got members of our own congregation who could benefit from a combination nursing and retirement home."

"Kind of a One Soul House." Ox thought about that. "We would have to do a lot of planning, and Hosanna left us enough money to invest in it. It's a thought, but that's long range and doesn't help us as far as Rebecca is concerned right now."

When Ox got back to his office and walked by Angel's office, he called out, "Angel, get Nathan Gibbs on the phone for me."

As he settled behind his desk, she buzzed. "He's on the line."

CHAPTER NINE

Nathan Gibbs was delighted to hear of Ox's interest. "Our Nursing Home Watch Program is in full swing. We have a number of members who are deeply concerned and devote hours every week. We are convinced we have saved a few lives. These nursing home people need to know they are being watched."

Ox told him about the experience with Night and Day Nursing Home.

"Well, I'll tell you what. Why don't we add them to our list? We'll visit Rebecca and ask to see Kitty Laker."

"Great. Maybe you and I should get together sometime to swap experiences. I'm thinking of starting a program here. In looking through the phone directory, I find there are more nursing homes than I can count."

"When our mutual schedules lighten up, we should meet and plan."

The following Monday, Ox and Elmer visited again. There were two aides on the floor. "That's a welcome addition," said Ox.

"Wonder what brought that on. Do you suppose our continued visiting had anything to do with it?"

"Maybe."

They walked into Rebecca's room and discovered two other visitors. One, a gray-haired woman, said, "One of you must be Reverend Christie. I'm Adelle Mitchell from the Unitarian Church. This is Florence Ebenbach," pointing to her companion. "Reverend Gibbs said we might run into you."

Rebecca seemed a bit more settled.

Elmer shook their hands and thanked them. "What you are doing for my great-niece is going to make a difference. There was only one aide on this floor before and half the time she wasn't here."

Miss Mitchell looked surprised. "There was only one out there when we came in."

"Well, there are two now, and that's a first."

Ox shook their hands also. "People like you keep the earth on an even keel. The world needs people like you and Reverend Gibbs."

"We've heard good things about your church," said Miss Ebenbach.

Miss Mitchell was holding Rebecca's hand. She nodded.

"I'm glad to hear that," said Ox. "I'm going to step out and ask why patients are coming and going in Rebecca's room."

He walked up to the nursing station. Immediately, a new aide greeted him as though he wasn't the enemy or carrying a disease "Hi. I'm Edith. Can I help you?"

"Well, I know you've been asked this before, but is there any word on Kitty Laker?"

"Yes. We just learned she's in the infirmary and should be back soon. I'll run down and let Miss Rhine know." She headed down the hall.

Ox looked at the aide who had been there off and on before. "I'm glad to see you are getting some help."

"Yeah. I can use it."

That was the end of that conversation, but Ox could hear the new aide talking to Rebecca and the others as though she had just discovered a long lost relative. The regular aide had her back to him looking at the air down the side hall. On a sudden urge he decided to go up a floor to see what was up there. The stairwell was the other direction from the aide's gaze, so in he went. He walked up the stairs, being careful not to make any clanging noises on the metal strips across each step.

The third floor seemed a duplicate of the second. The nurse's station was unoccupied. He looked in all directions and saw no one. Except for a few moans, the floor was eerily quiet.

Slowly, he walked down the hall that ran above Rebecca's and glanced into each room. Beds seemed to be occupied by people who weren't moving or making any sounds. He stopped and peeked into one of the rooms. It was a double. In both beds there were sleeping men. They were old, wrinkled, and bald. Maybe this was a male floor. He hadn't thought about it, but he hadn't seen any men on the second floor. Well, there were some in the wheelchairs. He heard a door clang somewhere and decided to head back.

Walking down the steps, he decided to take a peek at the basement. It would also give Elmer more time to visit. The door was a heavy metal thing. He pushed it open cautiously. He could hear the hum of equipment. The hallways were lighted with exposed overhead bulbs, six to a fixture, but they were dim compared to the lighting upstairs. The place looked abandoned.

Farther down one hall, an opening off to the side cast a steady, flickering light. It was probably an open furnace. He heard someone whistling. It looked pretty run of the mill. Time to go back upstairs.

Coming out on the second floor, he found himself facing Edith. She smiled graciously and said, "Rebecca seems much happier. We are so glad she has visitors. So many of our residents have no one."

"Well, my church is thinking of starting a nursing home watch program so that some of those residents will have visitors and know that someone cares."

"How nice."

Ox thought he caught a glimpse of anger, but it flickered away immediately and Edith smiled.

"How very thoughtful."

Elmer came up the hall. "The ladies said they would be back again this week. That takes a little burden off of me."

Ox wasn't sure about the burden being lifted.

Driving home, he thought he saw a car following behind him the entire way.

That evening, at the Rapid Creek Nursing Home, Buck Washington and Jamail Thomas were finishing their ten-hour shift. They were both big men and always together. They might as well have been conjoined twins. They walked down to the second floor and down the halls looking for "opportunities." There were no purses, wallets or checkbooks in sight. Most of the residents learned, but there were always those beyond learning.

Ann Cooke saw them and stood up as though to say "I'm watching you." They laughed. "Why don't you come home with us and have some fun, or are you too good for us because you been to college?"

"Don't do anything on my floor."

"You come with us and we do something with you on the floor." This was pretty much a nightly ritual.

They walked down to the first floor and past the administrator's office, now empty. Going out the front door they spoke to Willis Taylor, the guard. "Take care, old man, and don't let no thieves in while we gone."

"Yeah, that wouldn't do—they might not leave you anything."

"Better watch your mouth 'fore we leave you in the alley."

Willis could hear them laughing as he closed the door behind them and stood looking out at the noisy night. He knew they would, too. One of these days, they would go too far.

Ox sat on the couch in the living room and relaxed. Barbara was getting dinner ready. He could hear her in the kitchen. This was the time to clear his mind of problems of the day. He loved dinnertime with Barbara and the kids.

Barbara was talking to Billy. "I told you to wash those dirty hands. They look like you dipped them in mud. How could you get them so dirty? You can't eat with those hands."

There were more kitchen noises with pots and dishes. "Martha, go tell Daddy dinner's ready. No, wait. Let me see those hands again, Billy." A few seconds later she said, "How could you get just the fronts clean and keep the backs so dirty?"

"I only eat with the fronts."

"Go wash the backs and the fronts."

Ox felt totally relaxed. He looked at his hands. He wanted to wash just the fronts, but he didn't know how. His son was a genius.

CHAPTER TEN

Ox kept Tuesday open so he could run over to the nursing home without Elmer. Elmer seemed to be feeling a little better about the place, but Ox knew something was just too pat.

What really seemed strange was the limited staff for such a big place. There were now two aides on Rebecca's floor plus the receptionist. The two orderlies, Link Unger, and the nameless big doctor wandered in and out. Starky was more evident. There was also the man who had gathered up the trashcans outside. Maybe he was from a maintenance department. The third floor seemed deserted as far as staff was concerned. He hadn't seen anyone in the basement, although he had heard whistling. There just weren't enough people for such a big place.

Pulling into their parking lot, he saw a car that looked suspiciously like the one that stayed behind him all the way home. He wondered if he was getting paranoid. He walked back to the "off-limits" building.

Link seemed less stressed. Evidently, Ox had won his trust.

"Just so you know, Link, Miss Starky really is a nice person underneath. She just has a difficult job. I want you to go upstairs with me. You spend all your time down here and that's not right.

You should be familiar with the whole building. After all, you are responsible for it."

"Are you sure it's okay?"

"Absolutely." Ox was sure the angels would forgive him for the little lie. It was for a good cause.

"Well, okay."

They had just reached the staircase when the front door swung open and an unfamiliar man walked in. He was short and stocky in build with a large head and pointed ears. He wore a large diamond tie tack indicating money.

"We thought we saw your car out there. I'm Joe Bush, the assistant administrator. What are you doing back here? You know this building's off-limits." He turned to Link Unger. "If we ever see you talking to this man again, you are history."

Ox said, "Actually he was just reminding me the building is off-limits. Said he isn't even allowed up these steps. I just dropped by to say hi. I'm getting ready to visit Rebecca Rhine."

"She's already had two visitors today. What are you up to? Getting your whole stupid congregation intruding on us?"

"Actually, there are two members of the Philadelphia Police Department in the congregation. Would you like for them to visit?"

"Take my advice. Keep your nose out of our business."

"Is visiting a patient intruding on you in some way?"

"Just be aware, we know where your church is, and your family."

Bush turned and held the door open. A large diamond ring on his hand reflected the sunlight.

"Mr. Bush, that sounds very much like a threat."

"The boss doesn't like interference."

"I'll drop up to see Miss Rhine."

"You do that and then don't come back here again."

Ox walked to the front and then decided to sit in his car and think about what had just happened. There was no longer any question—something was rotten in Denmark. He had been there only a few minutes when Joe Bush rounded the corner pushing Link Unger in front of him. Link looked scared out of his wits. They didn't glance in his direction, but went directly into the building. A few second later, Joe Bush stepped back out and glared in Ox's direction. Ox ducked down. When he peeped out, Bush was gone. The receptionist must have told him Ox hadn't come in.

Ox decided he would leave. He couldn't take any threats against his family. This called for a different tactic. He started the car and headed back to the church. They would definitely start a nursing home watch program. He would do a sermon on it.

He glanced in the rearview mirror. It didn't appear he was being followed. He stayed in the slow lane and found himself in a line of traffic stopped for a UPS truck. Cars in the left lane zipped past. One was the car from the parking lot.

The truck finally moved and now Ox was in a hurry. He decided to go home before going back to the church.

CHAPTER ELEVEN

Ox pulled up in front of the house. The nursing home car wasn't in sight. He felt relieved.

Walking in the front door he called, "Anybody for a snack?"

Barbara was standing in the living room. "Hush, you big-mouthed preacher. The children are napping."

"Oh, yes. I forgot about nap time."

"Why are you home this time of day? Get fired?"

"What kind of a terrible person would ever fire a minister?"

"A really terrible person. Meet any lately?"

Ox told her about his encounter at the nursing home. "You came home because you were worried about us."

"Well, maybe I'm overreacting. Ministers are allowed to overreact."

"What are you going to do now?"

"My sermon this Sunday is going to be about people life has deserted in nursing homes. I want to get volunteers to visit people in those places. As Nathan Gibbs said, 'those places need to be watched.'"

"Maybe we ought to start our own nursing home in Hosanna's old mansion."

"That's amazing. Elmer and I talked about the same thing. The problem is it would require all kinds of staffing."

"It could be a rest home for members of our congregation and members of the other churches in our movement."

"Well, it's something to think about in the future. Right now, I've enough on my platter."

"Yes. Right now we have to watch out for Mr. Bush."

Back at the church, Ox went to work on his sermon. He thought of Emmett and Jessie May. Sunday, he would approach them to get the police involved, if possible. Their sergeant, Oster, was like a bulldog. If he got started, he'd never let go. He could be obnoxious, but maybe that was what it would take. Diplomacy was out of the question. He would also file a complaint with the state, for whatever good it would do. He would establish a system of review to keep an eye on the nursing home. A broader goal would include all nursing homes. He would continue to drive Elmer over, but he would keep away otherwise. His work would have to be behind the scenes. At least Elmer was less worried, but that might not be a good thing. The third floor had been almost too quiet. It was like a morgue. Joe Bush didn't look like any assistant. He seemed to just suddenly be there.

Ox mumbled to himself, "Who is he? Why did he suddenly appear?"

Angel tapped on Ox's door. "Ox, can I see you for a few minutes?"

"Of course, Angel. Is there a problem?"

"I don't know if I'm going crazy, but I have to talk to somebody. I think I can with you. You are the best person I have ever known."

"Well, Angel, that's truly a nice compliment. You are a good person yourself, you know."

"As you know, I'm alone. It's been that way . . . for some time, and it's going to be that way for the rest of my life." She looked confused. "Well, I don't know why I said that. That's not the problem. The problem is that I've had bad dreams. I hear screams, but they come out of the dark . . . just screams. Every night. It's been going on for a while now. They frighten me." She stopped and then said, "I thought you might have a suggestion."

Ox realized she just needed to tell someone. "Angel, you are a sweet, good person. If it's a ghost of your past, it's just that and nothing more. Talking about it might remove the fear or apprehension. From now on, every morning, tell me how many screams you heard."

"I should count them?"

"Exactly."

"I don't know if I can."

"You'll find you can. Just try it."

Not far from Night and Day Nursing Home, Joe Bush relaxed in his office. The room had no windows. He liked it that way. He could be there and no one else could know. He liked his privacy. He could spend hours here without interruption. During the day, his secretary was there, but she never interrupted. He answered his own phone. She was for looks. She could warn him if someone was in the reception area. His car was parked in one of the private garages in the basement.

He spent hours reviewing nursing home websites, those that had them. At six o'clock, his secretary brought in dinner and left. While he ate, he studied the websites of jewelry stores. After that he went back to studying the state website for nursing homes, the Department of Human Services, and especially the State Operations Manual. It was necessary to know the rules in order to evade them.

He made lists of areas the state might examine in their periodic surveys. He listed those nursing homes with the most apparent problems, those most likely to fail. The Group would be interested in possible acquisitions or maybe relieving troubled homes of some of their "free" patients. The Group homes were near capacity. Bush kept it that way, but there was always room for a patient with the right qualifications. The Group relied upon him. He had the time to do the research. It was his only interest.

He worked on the books for The Group's homes. He reviewed patient records and made appropriate changes to assure state approval. It was necessary to pass the silly state inspections.

He thought of Oxford Christie . . . the fly in the ointment. There was always some problem he had to get rid of.

CHAPTER TWELVE

The church was filled. When Ox had first come to the Church of the One Soul, there were only the old members, or as Barbara referred to them, the remains. Now the new members outnumbered them by three to one. It seemed preposterous to think it, but the congregation might outgrow this enormous building. He wondered if he should have two services each Sunday, one at nine and one at eleven. Actually, more members meant more possible volunteers for a nursing home watch program. He took his place at the podium.

"We live in a world where good people have to keep evil in check or it will spread like a cancer. Greed corrupts the minds of the weak. It's not enough that we fight to keep ourselves free of this cancer of the soul. We need to fight it at every corner of our lives. The world is flooded with many forms of evil. Greed leads the spiritually disabled to destroy the lives of others for personal gain. It morphs into many forms: theft, embezzlement, robbery, and murder, to mention just a few. On a broader scale, it brings about wars and unacceptable customs. We've seen it in this country with slavery and its cousin, racial discrimination. The Civil War was based on that and personal power and wealth. Congress has had vested interests all the way back to the Civil War with some members of Congress actually engineering Confederate victories by withholding troops from unpopular Union generals. It's amazing the North won. And think of the Holocaust. This is not a nice world where children, women, the elderly are mercilessly killed.

"Today, I want to focus on one particular form of this evil and a possible way for us to help stop it. The subject is nursing home abuse. Right now, at this very moment, there are helpless people being slowly tortured in nursing homes. They are subject to the worst kind of neglect—neglect on purpose. They are abandoned. They lie in their own waste without nourishment for days while the owners collect payments from Medicare and Medicaid and use the money for themselves rather than for the care of the patients. Staffing is inadequate. Some of the staff is incompetent, putting even more burdens on the competent. The owners want to keep the patients alive so they can continue to collect the payments so they do just enough, but no more.

"I witnessed one patient being transferred to a hospital. He was covered with bedsores from weeks of lying in his own waste. He was dehydrated from lack of liquids and from diarrhea. He was dying and in constant burning pain from the bedsores. The driver of the ambulance was disgusted. He told me he was constantly taking nursing home patients to the hospital to be brought back to life through intensive treatment only to be transferred right back to the nursing home where the process would start all over again. This was at one nursing home. Multiply that by the multitude of nursing homes in the Philadelphia region."

"The Germantown Unitarian Church has developed a nursing home watch program. Members of the congregation volunteer to visit nursing home patients, especially those who have no relatives to check up on them. Nathan Gibbs, the minister, stated flatly, 'Those places need to be watched.' I am having discussions with him regarding their procedures. I am hoping maybe we can develop such a program here. Imagine if every church developed nursing home watch programs.

"The state falls down on nursing home quality of care. They inspect them, but they let them know when they are coming to inspect, giving them time to hide what they are doing. We need to act. The angels can't do it all. They need the help of all good people. It is necessary for good people to keep evil in check or it will spread like a cancer."

Ox didn't mention he suspected something clandestine taking place in the Night and Day Nursing Home. That building with the green windows was hiding something. What?

In the reception line after the sermon, a number of members said to count them in. At the coffee hour, Cynthia Neal came over.

"I'd like to arrange concerts for nursing home patients. My students would love it. It would not only be good for the patients, it would help round out my students."

"It would seem to me we could arrange something."

"I could have them play old favorites, maybe seasonal pieces. It's obvious what we would play in December, but other seasons offer possibilities. There's Thanksgiving in November. There's Easter. We could play a mixture of religious and secular works, old favorites, music from their earlier years. I would have my students research the most likely music through the decades. It would be violin music since they are, after all, with the String Instrument Society."

"You've really given this some thought."

"My parents are old. I can imagine them in a nursing home if something happens to me."

* * *

Ox was tired. It had been a full day and then some. At dinner that night, everyone was quiet. It was as though they all sensed his exhaustion. They continued to sit at the table without talking after the meal. Ox looked at his family. Martha was growing up. She definitely had a mind of her own. Billy had already shown signs of independence. Ox felt a need to liven things up.

"It's time you kids knew the truth about your father."

That brought them to life. Barbara rolled her eyes with a "what now" expression.

"My name's not really Oxford Christie. It's Prince Manuel Frobischer III, but you mustn't tell anyone. It's a secret. I had to leave my country because there were people who would harm me."

Martha immediately looked skeptical. She knew her father. "Oh, yeah? What's the name of the country?"

"Frobischer Land. It's way up north."

"Oh, yeah? What's the flag look like?"

"It's all white like snow with rabbit tracks running from the upper right corner to the lower left corner. There's nothing but snow up there and there are rabbits running everywhere. Now you mustn't tell anyone, because there are people looking for me and we might all have to move to Frobischer Land, and you wouldn't like all that snow. It's cold."

"Oh, yeah? Well, I'm going to go out and tell everyone you are Prince Manuel Frobischer III."

Billy looked deeply offended. "Well, I'm going to go out and tell everyone you aren't." That did it. Ox and Barbara dissolved in laughter, thinking of Billy going around the neighborhood telling everyone his father wasn't Prince Manuel Frobischer III. That certainly livened things up.

Barbara looked at her husband and said, "You're a piece of work."

"Shh. Don't tell anyone."

Ox felt better.

CHAPTER THIRTEEN

Angel tapped on Ox's door. She had been checking in with him ever since her discussion about the screams. "I only heard four screams. They don't frighten me anymore."

"Only four. That's the smallest number yet. Soon, you may not hear them at all."

"I owe it to you. Counting them made them less frightening." She went back to her office.

Ox was glad he had been able to help her. It had been a lucky guess that counting would remove the unknown from the screams. He hadn't mentioned it to Barbara. She majored in psychology. He would share it with her. It wouldn't be breaking a confidence if he didn't tell her who it was. Barbara and he were two halves of a whole.

Ox chauffeured Elmer for the next visit, but stayed in the car. He parked on the far side of the lot and looked at the green-windowed structure.

A pickup truck pulled up outside the secret building. Two men unloaded a large metal drum, which was obviously heavy. They got it down and rolled it into the building. After a while, they came back out. One of them was carrying the drum, now obviously empty. He put it back into the truck, and then they repeated the process with a second drum. Before they came back out, heavy smoke billowed from the building's chimney. Ox guessed the contents of the drums were being incinerated. Strange that they brought something from the outside to be incinerated here. He hadn't seen the truck before. It didn't have the nursing home's name on it. The two men stood by the truck watching the smoke. After a while, they leaned against the side of the truck and lit cigarettes as though watching the black billowing mess prompted a like action.

The Group met in Susan Starky's office. Miss Starky wasn't present. She had been excused. There were six men. One of them was Joe Bush. They all had diamond rings and diamond tie tacks. It was as though they all belonged to the same fraternity. The man with the pear-shaped head conducted the meeting.

"Is Starky still doing as she's told?"

"She's still under control," said Bush. "She'll do as she's told. She knows she better. We had a slight problem with a visitor at North and South, but that seems to be resolved."

"All right, let's look at the figures. You've all been given a finance packet. Our gross this past month was a record, a little over six million . . . net, five and a half mil. Gentlemen, the process is beginning to pay off. We can all live in the style to which we are entitled. We've earned it. If we want to continue to earn it, we have to operate under close security. Mr. Bush, let us know if there are any problems we should know of."

Elmer strolled out of the building and made his way to Ox's car.

"Rebecca has had visitors every day this week. Kitty Laker is back. She's very withdrawn and doesn't talk. Just moans a little and turns her head away from everybody."

"Rebecca hadn't described Miss Laker as being reclusive. I got the impression she had been friendly."

"Yes," said Elmer. "Rebecca says she has changed. Maybe she has been sick and needs time to recover."

"That's possible."

Ox was about to start the car when a long gray limousine pulled up to the front entrance of the home. He watched. No one got out. Then, six men came out of the building. The "receptionist" held the door for them. One of them was Joe Bush. He was the third to duck into the limousine.

As the limo pulled away, he saw Miss Starky standing just inside the front entrance. "That was interesting," said Elmer. "They sure didn't look like visitors."

"Not by a long shot."

That night after the children were in bed, Ox told Barbara about Angel's screams without mentioning it was Angel.

"Wow. You missed your calling Dr. Freud. That was brilliant. She's curing herself, thanks to you."

"It's a matter of facing our goblins."

"You having her count the screams made the whole thing objective, removing the unknown, putting her in control. Rats, I thought I was the one who majored in psychology. I think you could have taught the course."

"Well," said Ox, "You're just saying that because it's true."

CHAPTER FOURTEEN

The State Society of Nursing Home Administrators met in Pittsburgh, near the airport. Joe Bush with six administrators from The Group's nursing homes attended, sitting in the back with instructions to listen and keep their mouths shut.

The president of the Society, a Mr. Bob Markson, was stressing the need to maintain high-quality standards. "Nursing homes get a bad rap because a few bad apples perform poorly. It's up to all of us to change that image. Quality care has to be the absolute bottom line."

He yammered on and on. There were some in the audience who really cared, but for others, attendance was only a P.R. necessity. For them, it was a long and boring meeting. They would go home feeling they had done their duty.

The Society met annually, rotating location from west to east to in between for the convenience of members.

Susan Starky paid rapt attention for the benefit of Joe Bush, who watched all six of them. She felt like a total imposter because of a lack of education for the job. She was just a messenger, and did as directed. She worried about where her parents were and if they were being cared for. They might not even be alive. She had no way of knowing, but simply had to do as told.

Susan wondered what hold The Group had on the other five. Bush was sitting in the aisle seat. She was six seats away from him. She wished she was farther. In between sat five people she hardly knew. Everyone had name tags that listed their nursing homes. She felt like hers was a lie. "Susan Starky, Administrator, Night and Day Nursing Home."

The others:

"Wally Mockler, Administrator, The Clouds Nursing Home," "Louis Giardinelli, Administrator, Healthy Acres Nursing Home," "Carlene Lambert, Administrator, Sheltering Pines Nursing Home," "Susan Manierie, Administrator, Angel Bed Nursing Home," "Boyd A. Silver, Administrator, Rapid Creek Nursing Home."

She did know one thing about Silver, his nickname was Trap Jaw. He had a hard demeanor to cover his incompetence and stupidity. She felt she was no better. She was out of place.

What was she to do? They gave her no budget to run the home on. She was more like a guard, watching to make sure nothing went wrong. There was hardly any staff working there. The patients were all dying. The Rhine girl was the exception. Humphrey called her when her uncle came in with her. She'd simply assigned her a room. Later, Joe Bush did the paperwork. All the other patients were transfers from the other nursing homes. Bush transferred them in when they met the criteria. The poor souls. Well, they'd lived their lives. She had hers to live. The Laker woman fooled them. She had seemed to regain her faculties after the transfer.

The good thing was that they didn't have visitors, except the Rhine girl. It was fortunate the girl had hallucinations. No one would believe anything she said. But now that Christie person seemed to be arranging visitors. He could be a problem. A threat to operations, to herself, and her parents.

She became aware there was a different speaker—the head of

the Awards Committee or something. He called a Mr. Robert Lawson of Reed Grove Nursing Home to the podium.

Lawson looked like a professional. Reed Grove received the Meritorious Award for Excellence. The state had not only found no defects, they found a long list of extra effort on behalf of the patients and their families. They got patients involved in multiple activities commensurate with their abilities. They were given activities to keep them mentally agile. The death rate was lowest of all the nursing homes. There were counseling programs not only for patients, but for family members. There were no charges beyond Medicare or Medicaid. There were beds available for patients with no coverage. The list went on and on.

Susan felt totally inadequate. Worse, she felt like a criminal.

Ox met with Emmett and Jessie May.

"Are either of you aware of complaints or problems with nursing homes?"

"Only if someone's grandmother is mistreated," said Emmett.

"Not often," said Jessie May. "We've followed up with meetings with administrators and nurses. Hard to prove anything. Nursing homes are notorious for poor record keeping."

"I'd really like it if you two could be involved in the Nursing Home Watch Program. If you visited in uniform, it could have a positive effect."

"You want us to visit Elmer's niece?" asked Jessie May.

"Her or her roommate, Kitty Laker."

"We'll find a way," said Emmett.

"It might be a good idea for me to fill you in on some of the things going on over there."

Ox told them about Susan Starky, the almost nonexistent staffing, the green-windowed building, the big doctor, the comings and goings of Kitty Laker, the truck unloading drums and the incinerator, the graveyard, the strange receptionist, and, of course, Joe Bush and his threat.

"I'll run a check on Susan Starky and Joe Bush," said Emmett. "There might be some history."

"It might be interesting to find out where that truck with the drums comes from. I can't say this is a police issue, but maybe we can check it out as church members. We better make it quick or Oster might begin to wonder what we are doing," said Jessie May.

"Do you think that Bush guy was serious about his threat?" asked Emmett.

"It gave me a jolt, especially since a car followed me home. I was concerned about Barbara and the kids."

"I'm going to make him my project," said Emmett.

"You make Bush a project, and I'll take on Starky," said Jessie May.

"I can't tell you how good it makes me feel that you two are involved. There's something creepy going on there."

After Emmett and Jessie May left, Ox called Barbara to see how things were. "Billy wants a pet pig. Martha's disgusted."

"How did you handle that?"

"I told her to tell him she wanted one, too. He'd lose interest."

"Did it work?"

"I think so. He's thinking of something else now."

"Don't mention goats."

Elmer dropped in. "They're doing some renovating at Night and Day, closing in the balcony with glass paneling. Starky will still be able to look out, but looks like some kind of meeting room or classroom."

CHAPTER FIFTEEN

Emmett and Jessie May cruised by Night and Day Nursing Home and spotted a pickup truck by the back building. They drove on past and came back. They stopped across the street, watched the unloading of the drums and the smoke billowing from the huge chimney. The two men leaned against the truck and smoked. They didn't seem to have a worry in the world. After a while they got into the truck and headed for the exit. Emmett and Jessie May followed at a distance.

"It would be better if we were in an unmarked car," said Jessie May.

It didn't matter. The guys in the truck were busy talking. Apparently, they weren't in the habit of looking in the rearview window.

Emmett and Jessie May followed the truck all the way to southwest Philadelphia. The truck stopped in front of Rapid Creek Nursing Home. The men got out and carried an empty drum into the building.

Emmett and Jessie May drove on past. After a few blocks, they turned around and came back slowly. They parked a block away and watched the two men drag a drum out and load it into the truck. They got in, turned around in mid-street and left.

Again, Emmett and Jessie May followed at a distance. The truck eventually wound up in South Philadelphia, stopping in front of The Clouds Nursing Home. The two men replaced another drum, and off they went.

"Must be the only thing these two do all day," said Emmett.

"We better report back in," said Jessie May. "Oster is going to wonder what we are up to."

"Maybe we should talk to him about the shenanigans."

"Right."

Emmett didn't start the car. He was thinking. "Let's go visit Elmer's niece."

"In uniform."

"Might create a reaction."

"Good idea. Oster can wait. Maybe we'll have something more to report to him. He can be stubborn."

Forty minutes later, they pulled into the Night and Day parking lot. They sat for a few minutes, giving anyone inside a chance to see them. They got out and walked rapidly to the entrance. When they came through the door, the strange looking receptionist stood up. Jessie May saw a figure dart away from the balcony above.

Emmett stared at the receptionist. "Which room is Rebecca Rhine in?"

"She's in 223. Is anything wrong?"

"We'll find out."

They went up in the elevator, leaving the receptionist standing. The aide was surprised and didn't say anything.

They walked into Rebecca's room. She was alone. They introduced themselves as friends of her uncle.

"We were in the neighborhood and thought we'd just drop in," said Jessie May. "Is everything okay?"

"Yes, except they keep taking my roommate away. I think she is sick. I hope she's not going to die."

"Let's hope not," said Emmett.

"We'll hope for the best," said Jessie May. "Is there anything we can do for you?"

"No. Everything's fine now. They've even put the call button where I can reach it."

Susan Starky stood in her office. She didn't know what to do. Why were the police there?

Were they coming to her office? What was going to happen? After a while, she realized she should be investigating. She opened her door, peered out, saw no one, and ventured out. She stepped back in and called the receptionist.

"What did the police want?"

"They're visiting the Rhine girl."

Starky didn't know whether to be relieved or more worried. Now what? What if Bush found out?

When Emmett and Jessie May came back out, they saw the pickup truck in back again. "Let's go back there and shake them up," said Jessie May.

The men watched them come, but didn't seem concerned. "What are you men unloading here?" said Emmett.

"Trash from the other nursing homes."

"What kind of trash?"

"Beats me. Whatever."

Jessie May noticed a large man in greens standing inside the door to the building. He moved away when he saw her looking at him.

"That must keep you guys busy," said Emmett.

"It's a living."

* * *

When Ox came out of the church, he saw a car that looked like the one that had followed him parked down the street. He couldn't be sure it was the same one. Was he being paranoid?

CHAPTER SIXTEEN

Ox was elated. Eleven members of the congregation had volunteered to visit. He decided he would ask Starky for names of other patients at Night and Day, patients who had no friends or relatives. Rebecca Rhine and Kitty Laker were already the recipients of a stream of visitors and he knew that would continue. Still, he worried about Kitty Laker. She seemed to be going through some kind of problem. Maybe he should suggest she be hospitalized. At the same time, he was worried if he interfered, there would be some kind of retaliation. He was torn. He weighed doing what he considered the right thing against threats to his family.

He lunched with Barbara and the kids and discussed the problem in terms the kids wouldn't understand. "I'm a bit concerned about a BushBush with the current course of action."

"Don't worry about a BushBush. Do what you know is right. The fact is, you don't have a choice."

He had known that was what she would say. He knew he really didn't have a choice.

Still . . .

At three p.m., he drove over to Night and Day. There was another car in the lot. He wondered if it was a visitor to see

Rebecca. He would drop in to see her after talking to Starky. He waved to Starky as he entered the building. She looked startled and waved back as though brushing away a fly. He walked over to the receptionist.

"I'm here to see Ms. Starky."

"She's not in."

"She just waved to me."

"Oh."

Ox headed for the elevator. On the second floor, he walked to the balcony area. It had been closed in with glass paneling and was now set up like a meeting room with rows of chairs and a table with a podium at the far end. Starky was not at her usual post. He knocked on her door. After a minute, she opened it and stepped out.

"I'm really rather busy. What can I do for you?"

"This should only take a few minutes. As you no doubt know, members of my church want to visit nursing home patients, especially patients who would normally receive no visitors. Being forgotten by the rest of the world has to be a terrible feeling. I wonder if you could give me the names of patients who receive no visitors."

Starky looked like she had been hit by a train. She actually gasped. She stepped back against the door as though to get away.

"No. No. No. I can't do that. Don't ask. It's not . . . it's not . . . allowed. I can't."

"It's really not asking much," he said. "I just want names of people you feel would benefit from having visitors."

"Please, no. Don't get me in trouble. I can't do that. You don't understand. It's wrong. I can't. I won't." Starky looked like she had seen a ghost. "They won't let me. I mean I can't. No. Company policy." Suddenly, she opened her door, darted in, and slammed the door shut.

Ox heard the lock click. He tapped on the door. "Miss Starky?" He stood there for a few minutes. He thought he could hear crying. After a few minutes, he decided to go see Rebecca.

Kitty Laker was back and seemed a little more cogent. Rebecca was sitting up. "We just had three visitors from the Philadelphia String Instrument Society. It was Cynthia Neal and two of her students."

That was whose car he had seen in the lot.

Kitty Laker looked at him. "It's nice seeing you again. I didn't feel much like talking before."

"I'm glad to see you feeling better."

"I'm still not up to par, but give me time. They removed a diseased kidney."

"Well, that would certainly explain why you're not feeling well. I hope things will be okay from now on."

"Any more of my parts I'll keep, diseased or not."

Rebecca seemed excited. "Things are definitely getting better, and Miss Neal wants to have a concert for the patients. How can that be arranged?"

Ox thought of the closed in balcony. Perfect. Now he had a lever to force Starky's hand.

Susan Starky called Joe Bush. "Please. It's not my fault. Please don't blame me. I didn't give him any names. I don't know what to do. I'm doing the best I can."

CHAPTER SEVENTEEN

Joe Bush sat in his office. That woman would be the death of him yet. Why couldn't she handle that Christie creep? He would have to do it himself. It always fell on him. Well, he'd drive over to Night and Day and have a talk with her. It was obvious she panicked. That kind of behavior would just convince Christie all the more there was a problem. He had to put a clamp on it. The police visiting made it worse. If anything happened to Christie now, the police would be convinced something was wrong, unless he had an accident. He went down to the garage.

What a waste of time. He had transfers to arrange.

Driving over, he wondered if he should just replace Starky, but she knew too much.

Replacing required security measures, and developing loyalty wasn't easy. Besides, he owned her.

He pulled into the lot. He knew Starky would know he was there. She was always watching, and that receptionist was loyal to her. Someday he would have to take care of him. The only person he could trust was that quack Dr. Rosenfeld, and that was only because he was at the end of his rope. He needed a clean sweep, all new staff.

He noticed two cars parked in the lot. Visitors. That

meddlesome Christie. The idea of him asking for patient names. What was he trying to prove?

He opened Starky's door without knocking. She was sitting behind her desk, obviously waiting for him.

"Please, Mr. Bush, I'll do whatever you say."

"You didn't make him unwelcome enough."

"Tell me what to do."

"I'll let you know." He looked out the back window at the graveyard. What if. . . ?

When Bush left, he was deep in thought. He didn't notice the police car following him. All the way to his office, he thought of the incinerator, the crematorium process, no evidence. Christie wanted a tour of the building. Maybe it was time.

Emmett and Jessie May followed Bush back to his office.

"I don't believe it," said Emmett. "This used to be a police station."

"Does it still have a lockup?"

"Unless it got ripped out."

"Talk about irony," said Jessie May. "Here we are tailing a possible perp to a police station."

"Wait'll Oster hears."

"That's it. Now he'll want us to do the investigation."

"Great," said Emmett. "He'll probably get into it himself."

CHAPTER EIGHTEEN

In the Police Roundhouse, Sergeant Oster looked at Emmett and Jessie May as though they were cockroaches.

"Where the hell have you two been? Who told you to go heading off all over the city checking on some cockamamie nursing home?"

"Our minister asked us to check on it because he suspected foul play," said Emmett.

"Who do you report to, Hoagie Brain, me or your minister?"

"Sarge," said Jessie May, "we think there is a serious problem, and one of the leaders is using an old police station in the Northeast as his headquarters."

"That old police station? I was stationed there when I was a rookie. What's he doing there?"

Emmett told him everything Ox told them and about the truck, the drums, the incinerator, the smoke and the reaction when they visited.

"Sarge," said Jessie May, "something is really peculiar about the operation and they are linked to all those other nursing homes. It's not just one place. It's a widespread operation."

"Well, it does sound strange," said Oster. "Why don't the three of us pay a visit and see the reaction. Let's take two cars just to give an extra jolt. Maybe I'll assign an extra patrol near that church and the Christie residence. Can't hurt."

The two police cars pulled into the lot. When Oster walked into the front lobby, he looked down at the receptionist who was too flabbergasted to say anything.

"What's your job? You a guard or what?" Oster leaned over him.

"I'm the receptionist."

"Tell your boss we want to see her."

"Yes, sir." He picked up the phone and dialed. "The police are here to see you." He put the phone down. "Second floor. When you get off the elevator, turn right. Her office is halfway across the balcony. She's expecting you."

Oster led the way. The door was open. Starky stood behind her desk. "What can I do for you?"

"What's going on in this place?"

"Patient care. That's what we do."

"You go about it in a strange way. What's really going on here? I want the truth. Do I have to search the whole place?"

"Oh, my goodness. Do you have a search warrant?"

"Since when do we have to have a search warrant to visit a nursing home?"

"Who do you want to visit?"

"Everybody."

"Well, it's not visiting hours right now."

"Fine. We'll be back."

The three officers left the building.

"That ought to rustle up some action," said Oster.

Starky was on the phone to Bush. "There were three of them. I told them it wasn't visiting hours. The sergeant said they'd be back. He didn't say when."

"Damn," said Bush. "We've got to do something."

Jessie May called Ox and let him know what they had done.

Ox decided maybe he would pay another visit with Elmer. Maybe he would wander around and take a look at that graveyard. Elmer was ready.

When they pulled into the lot, Ox told Elmer he would be nosing around on the outside and he would leave the car unlocked in case Elmer got back before he did.

Ox crossed the lot and walked to the graveyard side of the building. There was a row of unmarked tombstones forming a border across the front of the graveyard. They looked like a low wall. The yard itself consisted of row upon row of metal markers, each with a small plastic container in back of it. The ground seemed undisturbed. Ox stooped to read the inscriptions. "Mary—June, 91."

"Joseph—January, 91." Row after row of little plaques with first names and dates.

"Can I help you?" It was Miss Starky.

"I was just curious about your graveyard."

"When they die, we cremate them, poor souls. They have no relatives. Nobody cares."

"It's really strange. Couldn't you at least give their last names?"

"We just think of them as our children."

Starky kept glancing up at the back window and Ox assumed that was where Bush was. "How long have you been working here?"

Starky seemed to give a nervous little jump at the question. "Well, a few years now. I feel dedicated."

"You don't have much staff for such a large place. Do you do the cremation here?"

"Yes, in our crematorium. They have no relatives, poor souls."

"Yes. Poor souls. No relatives or friends. No one to check on them. You have a clinic in that building?"

"It's a recovery unit. Off-limits to visitors."

"You mean it's a kind of intensive care unit?"

"No. It's a recovery unit for patients who are sicker."

"Well, why do you send a patient to a hospital for bed sores if you have a recovery unit?"

"They are too busy to handle anything that routine."

Starky was getting more nervous by the minute. It was obvious she wanted to get away.

She kept glancing up at the back window. Had someone told her to come down? "Is Bush an easy man to work for?"

"Oh, bosses are bosses."

"Did he tell you to get down here and get me out of here?"

"Oh."

"Well, I'll tell you what. I'll leave, but sometime soon, you and I will need to talk."

Ox turned and walked back toward the front of the building. He wondered if any good nursing homes existed. It was a while before Elmer came out.

CHAPTER NINETEEN

Joe Bush reported to the Group. "Things have gotten worse. Christie has gotten a string of visitors coming in from his church and now he's gotten the Unitarians involved. They could start visiting our other nursing homes as well. Now he's gotten the police involved. It's getting really serious. Our whole operation is being threatened. I wonder if we should slow down transfers and begin to operate in a more 'normal' way. Maybe they'll lose interest if things seem okay. I can't think of any other way right now. It's become too involved, out of control."

The man with the pear-shaped head said, "Hold the transfers, but this Christie has to be stopped. Take care of it."

One TV news program Oster hated was the D'Ablo news hour. Helen D'Ablo seemed to feel it her duty to attack public figures and government agencies. She frequently focused vicious attacks on the police. She haunted the police station, looking for suspects the police were abusing. Her police scanner was always running, picking up communications between headquarters and squad cars.

Her twin sister, Eleanor, assisted her. They were known as the devil twins. Scanning was almost a twenty-four-hour process. A younger sister, Louise, backed them up on the scanner.

Oster held them in contempt. They seemed to completely overlook the truth and either exaggerated or invented problems, like politicians describing opponents. The D'Ablos assumed the role of prodding those who didn't need it, always making themselves look important and vital to society. What they lacked in quality, they made up for in quantity.

Helen listened to a report on the scanner from Emmett about something going on at Night and Day Nursing Home.

"What are they up to now, fooling around with nursing home patients?"

"The police are all bullies. Those lost souls in nursing homes can't fight back," said Eleanor.

"Right. Easy victims. We'll do a report on them."

"Good thing we're here to keep the public informed," said Eleanor.

CHAPTER TWENTY

Angel answered the phone again. A man kept calling for Ox, but wouldn't leave a message. She was nice to him each time. It was just her nature. She wouldn't hurt a living creature. It even bothered her to kill a fly. She had a pet mouse named Jonathan. She left tidbits for it in a bowl she kept in a corner of her kitchen. Each morning, she would find the bowl empty. She had never seen Jonathan. For all she knew he could be a Jenny.

The man called again. "Doesn't he ever come in?"

"Well, he's very busy. He does a lot for other people."

"Well, I'm going to leave him a message. Tell him to mind his own business or I'll pay him a visit."

When Ox came in, Angel gave him the message. Ox was sure it was Bush. Feeling compelled to visit other nursing homes just for comparison, he decided to go through the phone book and call a few to see if he could just come in and look around. He might need to recommend a nursing home to some members of his congregation. He realized he was warning them ahead of time, but he would waste no time getting there after the phone call.

The first thing he noticed was that most did not refer to themselves as nursing homes.

The closest was nursing home and rehabilitation center. Some called themselves health centers or care centers. Some were called nursing centers. Well, at least they were listed under nursing homes. He decided to start at the top and work his way down the list.

The first one was answered by a woman who evaded him by saying they would have to know who the patient was so they could evaluate if they were the right facility for the individual.

Elmer came in as he hung up. When Ox told him what he was doing, Elmer said, "Why not take a few members of the Nursing Home Watch Committee with you? You've got to delegate some of this or you'll never get done."

"Good idea. I can use all the help I can get." He buzzed Angel. "Angel, please see if you can set up a meeting of the Nursing Home Watch Committee. The sooner, the better."

He closed the phone book. There was no point calling until they were ready to visit. He could see the light going off and on as Angel made the calls.

Elmer stepped over into her office. "Count me in."

Ox decided to invite Nathan Gibbs. He might have some valuable suggestions. He wondered what Bush meant by "I'll pay him a visit." Well, he'd give him reason to, but he might have to visit a lot of people. He decided to call Emmett and Jessie May and let them know. The dispatcher put him through and Jessie May answered.

"Just so you know," she said. "Oster has assigned an additional squad car just for your street. Not only that, he said he might start coming to church. I don't know if he feels you need protection during your sermon or what. I've learned not to question him."

Ox thanked her. He felt a little better. Oster was nobody to fool with. He wondered about him attending Sunday services.

Somehow, he didn't think Bush would be a danger there, but you never knew. At any rate, he needed to take a break to be with Barbara. He drove the few blocks and was passed by a police car on the way. He breathed a little easier.

Barbara said, "I want to be part of all those visits. I've been thinking of visiting Elmer's niece anyhow. I've even toyed with the notion of taking the kids with me. Is there any age restrictions for visitors?"

Ox said, "I don't know, but I'll check it out. The more questions I have for Starky, the better. In fact, that's a question for all the nursing homes."

CHAPTER TWENTY-ONE

Ox was working on his sermon when Emmett called.

"We've been checking on Starky. It's unusual to find zip on anyone, but we'll keep digging. We can't find anything about her parents. As far as we know, she has no siblings. As far as work experience, nothing. We'll keep digging."

Starky. Ox envisioned the woman. Somehow, he felt she would be the way into what was going on. She was obviously afraid of Bush. Why did she stay there? No other options? Poor work experience? Her face gave the impression she had led a hard life, as though what she had, she had earned the hard way, except it didn't add up. She wasn't self-sufficient at Night and Day. He would go see her again, maybe with Emmett and Jessie May.

Ox called them. They agreed to go with him to see Starky. When they wandered into the front lobby, the receptionist wasn't in sight. They went up to the second floor and tapped on Starky's door. It took a full minute, but she opened the door.

"We need to talk to you," said Ox. "It's important for us and for you. I think you know that."

Starky backed up. She looked like she wanted to run. Then she seemed to get hold of herself. "I'm afraid I don't understand."

"We think you are caught up in something you're not happy with."

"Not everyone is happy with their work. Actually, I'm very pleased with my work. I wouldn't have it any other way."

"You like working for Bush?"

"I like this work. I'm dedicated to it."

"I don't believe that."

"What did you want to talk about?"

"What we can do to help you."

"I don't need any help, thank you."

Jessie May stepped forward. "Can you tell us where your parents are?"

Starky almost collapsed. She grabbed the edge of a table. "I haven't seen my parents for some time."

Jessie May handed her a card. "If you decide you need help, please call.

Starky looked totally wrung out. She stuttered and then said, "Thank you. I'll keep the card. Now, I have work to do. Thank you."

Ox said, "Hope to hear from you."

When they walked through the lobby, the receptionist looked guilty. He had probably been on an illegal break.

In the police car going back, Jessie May said, "I think there's a possibility we'll hear from her."

Emmett said, "I don't know. She might really be satisfied with her work. It might be the only thing she can get. I don't think we can count on hearing from her. Maybe if we keep up the pressure. This might have been a dry run."

"I don't know," said Ox. "My instincts tell me she's the key. Bush wouldn't win a popularity contest with her right now."

"Well, did you notice her reaction when I asked about her parents? There was something strange about that."

"Maybe her parents disowned her," said Emmett.

Back at the church, Ox found Ellen Cullen, the Religious Education Chair, coming down the steps from his office.

"Oh, good," she said. "I had just about given up catching you today. I wanted to let you know that the teenagers, the Teen Souls, will be visiting different churches to learn and appreciate other people's religions and beliefs. It's part of our program to broaden the perspective of our younger members. Well, you already know that. I just wanted you to know that last week they visited your friend, Father Maloney's Catholic Church. This week it will be Lutheran. By the way, Maloney sends you his regards. He was really nice with our group, invited them to view the altar trappings close-up after the service. He also let them take a seat in the confessional."

"I'm glad it went well." Ox paused. "How did it go with the Ambruster boy? He tends to be a bit challenging."

Ellen nodded. "Rob initially said he intended to bob up and down like them. I explained to all of them it was our choice to visit them, so good manners requires us to follow their customs. It all went just fine."

"Good."

"After our Lutheran visit, we will stay in-house for a discussion. Then, the next Saturday, we will meet in the parking lot for a visit to the synagogue."

"Rabbi Kemelman is fairly new to our Interdenominational Clergy group, but he was receptive to our teen project. I'm sure he'll welcome our young people."

"Great."

"Thanks, Ellen. It's good to know our teens are learning to be accepting. So many people aren't, which is a shame given that this country was founded on religious freedom."

Ox decided he would add a note to his sermon about it.

CHAPTER TWENTY-TWO

Susan Starky leaned against the door. She could hear them walking away. What did they know? What was she going to do? She couldn't report this to Bush. How did all this happen? She felt sick. There was no place to turn. There was no one who could help. She couldn't leave. She couldn't stay. She couldn't do anything.

She walked to her desk and collapsed into her chair. She felt tired. She felt like she could sleep for a week. Maybe she would wake up and find this was all a bad dream. She didn't dare talk to Bush about it. He was too punitive. He would get mad, threatening. There had been too many threats. She didn't dare talk to the police. Could she be arrested? Maybe that would be better. The minister, Christie, what could he do? Pray for her? Bush would retaliate if she told anybody. The people on the staff, they were all stupid. Dr. Rosenfeld was a maniac. She had to raise hell with everyone just to keep things running and save her skin.

She thought of going to the police, but it was too much of a gamble. What could they do but just stir the pot and get Bush mad. That was the last thing she wanted.

She was trapped, trapped in this job and trapped in this building—cooped up in that third-floor room when she wasn't in the office. She hated the building. It was a jail.

That receptionist, Humphrey what's-his-name, would he report to Bush the police and Christie had been here again? She couldn't make him out. What had she done to deserve this? Her poor parents, what had they done?

Maybe she would talk to Christie, but she couldn't contact him. She would have to wait until he came back. Maybe she wouldn't.

CHAPTER TWENTY-THREE

Dr. Rosenfeld looked down at the elderly woman. She was completely bald. She opened her eyes and screamed.

"Not you again. Somebody get me out of here."

Dr. Rosenfeld clamped a mask over her mouth and nose. In less than a minute, she was asleep.

The Nursing Home Watch Committee met in the church community room. When Ox walked in, twenty people were already there, including Barbara. She had left the children with a babysitter. Nathan Gibbs came in through the outside entrance.

"Thanks, Nathan, for coming," said Ox.

"My pleasure. Are all these people part of your nursing home watch program?"

"Yes, there may be a few more coming."

"Well, ours is a project of the Social Responsibility Committee. They have a number of projects. You've outstripped us. We probably have eight or ten people."

"I met two of them at Night and Day Home. I'm sure you can give us some pointers."

"I suspect we'll be learning from each other."

The group sat in a large circle. Ox asked Gibbs how they made contact with nursing homes, how they got names of patients to visit.

"It varies," said Gibbs. "Some, of course, are members of our congregation. Some requests come in from people who have heard of our program. We visit some nursing homes and just walk into some patients' rooms. When we do that, we introduce ourselves and ask how they are being treated. Some nursing homes welcome us. Some don't like it. Those are generally the ones that need to be watched the most. We've even contacted other churches to ask if members of their congregations have suggestions or requests. We get some rejections because some think we are proselytizing for new members. We are very careful to never push our own religion on anyone. We've even contacted the State Health and Human Services Department, but got no help. They seemed officially unconcerned. I think they thought we were invading their territory. It might depend on who in that office you talk to. Some people get defensive. If you find flaws in a facility they've approved, they take it as a reflection on them. Anyhow, that's been our experience."

"Thanks, Nathan. We've been thinking of just calling to ask if we could just walk through. What's your perception of that approach?"

"As good as any, but go right away if they don't reject you. Get there before they can make things look better."

"Nathan, are there any really good nursing homes?"

"We've not found any that we would rank as really good. We found some that do a few things right, but that seems to be the result of an occasional employee with a conscience. Those employees don't seem to last. Doing things right can cost money and money is often the goal, not good care."

"Are there any nursing homes where you might like to see us involved?"

"One that comes to mind is Rapid Creek. Patients seem to get robbed. Security is lacking. We visit at least once a week, but the place definitely calls for more."

"Do your people always go in pairs?"

"Yes, absolutely. Sometimes you want morale support. There's always safety in numbers."

The conversation went on for close to an hour, the committee selected a chairperson and started working on a plan of action. Ox excused himself, and he and Nathan walked outside.

"Thanks for coming over. Your experience was valuable in getting the group developed."

"Thanks for asking me. Sometime I'd like for you to come over to Germantown to give us a progress report."

As Nathan drove off, Barbara joined Ox.

"If you visit one of the other nursing homes, let me go with you. We can take the kids. Talk about safety in numbers. The committee is going to be making the initial phone calls, so you don't have to do that."

"Good. I'd rather concentrate on Starky and Night and Day."

"I suggest you never go over there alone."

CHAPTER TWENTY-FOUR

Sergeant Oster went down into the police archives in the Philadelphia Roundhouse. He searched through the old records of Northeast Philadelphia until he found what he was looking for. He pulled out a box of records from the old police station.

He sat at a table and pulled out folder after folder. He opened one and spread the contents out on the table. There it was—the blueprints of the old building, including the office, the lockup, and the garage, all of it. In a small container were keys to fit all the locks. He slipped them into his coat pocket.

Ox had kept his calendar clear for the afternoon. He had some misgivings about it, but Barbara talked him into it. The whole family was going to visit Rebecca. He stepped into Angel's office.

"Angel, I'll be gone for the rest of the afternoon. Lock up when you leave. I'll see you tomorrow."

"I'm worried about you going over there. I don't think it's safe."

"Nothing's going to happen in broad daylight, especially with the kids."

"I don't know."

* * *

Ox really was worried, not for himself, but for Barbara and the children. Maybe Bush wouldn't be there. He was the one to worry about. At least he assumed there was no one else to worry about.

Martha and Billy were strapped into their car seats in the back of the car. "We make a delightful little family to be visiting at a nursing home."

"Maybe delightful to some."

There was another car in the visitors' parking lot. "Good," said Ox. "Safety in numbers."

"You suppose someone else is visiting?"

"It's the visitors' lot."

"Does anyone other than Rebecca get visitors?"

"I doubt it." Ox pulled close to the entrance and they went through the process of unbuckling belts and putting little feet on the pavement.

"Stay close to us," said Barbara. "What a huge building." She added, tongue in cheek, "I wonder if there are any secret passages."

"I think the whole place is a secret passage." He thought to himself, a passage to somewhere.

The receptionist looked totally surprised when they walked in. He stood up and then sat down. He didn't say a word as Ox and his menagerie walked toward the elevator.

Ox said, "We're visiting Rebecca Rhine." The receptionist nodded.

Martha and Billy stared at him as though he was something from a picture book. "He's a giant," said Billy.

Barbara held his hand and they walked a little faster. The children became excited when the elevator door closed behind them and groaned up to the second floor. The patients sitting in the wheelchairs didn't notice, but the aide actually smiled.

They found Florence Ebenbach and Adelle Mitchell in Rebecca's room. Rebecca smiled when she saw the children.

"Oh, they're beautiful."

Ox introduced Barbara and the kids to the two visitors. "I'm Adelle."

"I'm Florence."

They both knelt down and kissed Martha and Billy. Billy wiped the kisses off.

While this was going on, Ox could see Rebecca's huge grin. He felt better about bringing the family. Barbara was right. It was like a party. He looked at Kitty Laker's empty bed but made no comment.

They stayed for half an hour and decided to leave before wearing out Rebecca.

In the hallway, Barbara said, "Okay, now I think we should visit your Miss Starky."

Ox was caught up in the mood. "Can't hurt." He pointed to the door to the balcony. "This way."

On the balcony, they found Starky at her usual post. She looked at the children, then the adults, then the children.

"Hello," she stammered. Her lips quivered. "How nice."

Ox could see how affected she was. Maybe it was a good sign. "We just wanted to drop in and say hello," he said.

Barbara gave her a hug. "You have a beautiful building."

Ox thought Starky was on the verge of crying, but she seemed to regain control of herself.

"We don't get many children visiting," she said.

Ox refrained from saying they didn't get many visitors, period. Then he remembered Cynthia Neal saying she might arrange a concert for the patients. He wondered what effect it could have on the souls in the wheelchairs.

"Miss Starky, one of our parishioners teaches violin at the

Philadelphia String Instrument Society. She would like to arrange a concert for your patients, and this balcony area would be ideal. What do you think?"

Starky seemed to be grasping for a response. "Maybe."

"We'll be in touch and make the arrangements. Would an afternoon be best?"

"Well, I guess afternoons." The idea obviously worried her.

Ox wasn't surprised. He was certain now she was the key to getting answers.

At Rapid Creek Nursing Home, two members of the Church of the One Soul, Hilda Danziger and Larry Pregle, met the administrator, Boyd Silver. Silver was not at all receptive.

"I don't like people intruding in my nursing home."

"I don't think you should call visitors intruders," said Miss Danziger.

"Who do you want to visit?"

Larry Pregle was annoyed by Silver. "We want to visit with people who are all alone in this world, people who don't get visitors."

"Maybe they don't want or need visitors, especially from some church group."

Hilda was polite to a fault. "We aren't here to preach. We just want them to know they aren't forgotten. You aren't going to keep us out, are you? You wouldn't do that, would you?"

Silver was obviously frustrated. "Go on in, but I'm too busy to waste time on you." He stepped back into his office and shut the door.

Miss Danziger was shocked. Pregle was angry. "Let's go on in."

They passed through double doors on the first floor and were shocked to see people sitting in a long line of wheelchairs. They looked like mannequins, just sitting without any expressions on their faces. Every one of them was bald. They walked down the patient unit and spotted an aide changing sheets on a bed.

The aide was surprised to see them. "Are you looking for someone?"

"Well," said Miss Danziger, "just anyone who doesn't get visitors."

"I'm surprised you got past the administrator." She said the word "administrator" as though it was excrement.

"I'm Hilda Danziger and this is Larry Pregle. We just want to let people know they aren't forgotten. A lot of people aren't able to get away to visit, and we just want to help."

"Well, there ought to be more people like you in the world. I'm Ann Cooke. I'm the nurse aide on this unit. We don't have much staff and I'm busy, behind with changing sheets, but I'll show you around." She tucked in another sheet corner and came around the bed to talk to them.

"There's only one person working on each floor. There should be a half dozen, but Mr. Silver wants to save money. Maybe your being here will make him see the light."

She led them down the hall past room after room with no patients. "They're in the wheelchairs until I can get the beds changed, assuming I have enough sheets."

Near the end of the hall, they found an occupied room.

"You can visit here. It'll be a while before I get down this far. This is Mr. Zimmerman and Mr. Cheek." She turned and left, but came back. "Good luck."

There were no chairs in the room. It was stuffy and smelled. The two men both lay in fetal positions, but one, Mr. Cheek, had his eyes open.

Miss Danziger knelt beside the bed. "I'm Hilda Danziger and this is Larry Pregle. We just wanted to be sure you were getting proper attention here."

"I'm Dan Cheek. Miss Cooke does the best she can, but she's only one person."

Larry Pregle knelt beside Hilda Danziger. "What's it like here at night?"

"Not good," said Cheek. "We keep our eyes closed."

His roommate opened his eyes. "Miss Cooke tries," he said.

"Is there anything we can do for you?" asked Hilda.

"Not anymore," said Cheek, "but thanks." He closed his eyes. His roommate's eyes were closed and the room was quiet.

The two visitors moved quietly out. They checked the next room. Two men were asleep. "Let's go upstairs," said Larry.

On the second floor, there were no wheelchairs. An aide sat at a small desk in a cubicle.

She stood up when she saw them.

"Is there something you're looking for?"

"We're just visiting," said Hilda.

"We don't get no visitors."

"Well," said Larry, "it's past time you did."

"Does Mr. Silver know you're here?"

"He said we could visit all we want to," said Larry.

"Well, that's never happened before. I've got a lot of work to do."

"Don't let us get in your way," said Hilda. "Can we help you?" The aide looked so surprised, Hilda laughed.

"Don't need no help."

"We'll just wander around," said Larry.

"I don't know if you should."

"Why not?" asked Hilda.

"Well, nobody's ever done that before."

"Then it's past time," said Larry.

He walked down the hall. Hilda followed. The aide just stood and watched. They entered the first room and the stench brought tears to their eyes.

"My Lord," said Larry.

Both patients were moaning. Hilda hurried back to the aide. "Those patients are hurting." She pointed at the room.

"Nothing I can do about it." The aide didn't get up.

Hilda went back to the room. Larry tried talking to the patients, but got no response.

Hilda and Larry didn't know what to do. If they left, they were abandoning two souls, but what could they do? Almost in a daze, they walked to the next room and found the same situation.

"We have to report this to the State," said Hilda. They left the "home" in a hurry.

CHAPTER TWENTY-FIVE

The day of the concert was a day of transformation at Night and Day Nursing Home, starting with the parking lot. Ox parked near the door. Barbara and the kids were with him. Larry Pregle and Hilda Danziger came with Elmer. Angel had gotten a volunteer to answer the phone. She brought two other members of the Nursing Home Watch Committee with her. Nine other members in three cars were there. Cynthia and her students came in two cars. In addition, Emmett and Jessie May parked but didn't come in. They sat in their car figuring their presence would be a plus as far as Bush was concerned. Bush's car was also in the lot.

Inside was more of a transformation. The patients in wheelchairs had been wheeled onto the balcony, appropriately up to the front area. There were thirty-two of them. There was evidence that a deodorizing spray had been used liberally to make the air more acceptable.

Cynthia and her six students sat in chairs up front. The other men, women, and children sat in the seats behind the wheelchairs. The aide, Edith, stood in back as though she were the monitor. The other aide stayed on the unit. Starky and Bush sat on the back row. Starky did everything but chew her fingernails. Bush glared at everybody.

At the last moment, Rebecca was wheeled in. She looked distressed.

Ox assumed by her expression Kitty Laker was still out. He wondered about the men on the third floor. The patients wheeled in were all from the second floor.

The violin music was music never heard in that building before. Cynthia had set up a program with a mix: classical, popular from fifty years ago, her own arpeggios, and a medley of seasonal songs ranging from New Year's Day through Christmas.

The concert was scheduled for an hour. When the Christmas music started, an amazing thing happened. Two of the patients in wheelchairs stood. They were singing. Then about half of the others began to sing. The song was "Silent Night."

Ox could see even those not singing were nodding and smiling. The violinists were overcome by the reactions and began to cry, but they kept playing. They repeated "Silent Night" over and over.

Ox's own eyes were wet and so were Barbara's. It was almost a miracle.

The music stopped and the patients all sat. They talked and laughed. Some of them cried.

Then one started clapping and they all did.

Ox thought Starky looked totally confused. Bush looked like he hated everybody. The patients were wheeled back into the hall where they became quiet once more.

Helen D'Ablo listened to the police scanner. Emmet, the idiot, as she called him, was reporting to Oster, whom she referred to as Adolph Hitler. So nursing home patients were being abused and the police weren't doing anything about it. What else was new? She would shake things up. Get them off their rear ends.

She called Eleanor from the next room. "We've got a report to prepare. First, we're going to pay a visit to a rotten nursing home, describe what we see, and report the police for letting it go on. People are being tortured and the police, as usual, are doing nothing. They are great at talking a good game."

"You're sure?" asked Eleanor.

"I'm sure. The police are worms."

CHAPTER TWENTY-SIX

Hilda Danziger and Larry Pregle reported to Ox. "It was awful," said Hilda.

"It's a terrible place," said Larry. "It ought to be closed down. Those people are criminals."

"Those poor souls were moaning. They just kept their eyes shut and took whatever came."

"The aide on the first floor seemed concerned, but the aide on the second floor just didn't give a hoot."

Hilda was almost in tears talking about it. "The administrator acted like we were intruders."

That reminded Ox of his conversation with the big doctor at Night and Day. "I think we need to pay a visit to the Health and Human Services Department in Harrisburg. Will you two go with me?"

"Absolutely," said Hilda. "When we left we were saying we needed to report them. The police ought to close them down. They're killing people through their neglect."

Ox called ahead to Harrisburg to make an appointment. The clerk transferred him to a supervisor when she heard what he wanted.

"We don't generally have time to talk to people about nursing homes. We're too busy monitoring them to prevent the need for complaints. Why don't you write us a letter, and the next time we inspect that facility, we'll follow up on it."

"No. This simply can't wait. There are lives at stake."

"Well, that sounds a little dramatic."

It was only through persistence that they were finally given an appointment.

They parked in a municipal parking garage, and after several wrong choices found the correct building. They were twenty minutes early, but Ox figured that would help them get in on schedule. He hadn't reckoned with the state method of operation.

They were ushered into a waiting room by an indifferent clerk. The appointment time came and went. When they waited thirty minutes past the appointment time, Ox left the waiting room, found another clerk and asked if they could please get in to see the supervisor of the Nursing Home Review Section.

"I'll let her know you're here."

After another fifteen minutes, a skinny blonde in a pantsuit came in. "I'm Miss Hahn. I understand you have a problem with a nursing home."

"Yes," said Ox. "Our church has a nursing home watch program, and we visited one that is obviously abusing patients."

"Yes. Well, let's go back to my office." She turned and headed down the hallway.

Hilda and Larry had to run to catch up. They entered an office with a large desk covered with stacks of papers.

She sat behind the desk. "Now, what can I do for you?"

Ox looked at Hilda and Larry. "Tell Miss Hahn about your experience at Rapid Creek Nursing Home."

Larry spoke up first. "We discovered patients moaning from pain, a whole floor of them, and the aide didn't do anything about it."

"Well, maybe the aide knew more about their conditions."

Hilda leaned over the desk. "Miss Hahn, they were all suffering and the aide said there was nothing she could do. She didn't care."

"Well, maybe she experienced that every day. Maybe she had already taken care of it."

"Miss Hahn, it was obvious that an entire floor of patients was being neglected. I think the state would want to know about it."

"Thank you. I'll make a note of it. Rapid Creek, did you say?"

"Yes. We think the state should investigate and put an end to this massive torture."

"We'll definitely investigate at our next scheduled survey. Now, if you don't mind . . ."

"Wait a minute," said Ox. "Did you say at your next scheduled survey?"

"Yes. We will definitely look into it. Thank you." She stood up.

"When will that be?"

"I would have to consult the schedule."

"You are saying that at some time off into the future, you'll check on them."

"Yes. We'll definitely check on them."

"All those patients could be dead by then."

"That's a bit melodramatic."

"They'll know when you are coming."

"That's the way it's done."

"Miss Hahn, that lets them clean up their act for the inspection."

"Hopefully, they'll continue to meet the standards."

"I have a suggestion. Don't tell them you're coming, and do it right away."

"What an interesting idea. We'll be in touch."

On the drive back, they were quiet.

The following day, Ox called Emmett and Jessie May. "Can you two go with me, Hilda, and Larry to Rapid Creek Nursing Home?"

"Name the time," said Jessie May.

In the following week, they pulled up in a police car in front of Rapid Creek. Boyd Silver looked up as they walked into his small office.

"What is it?" he asked.

Emmett leaned over Silver's desk. "We have reports of abuses taking place here."

"We give better care than most nursing homes. Our staff is trained."

Hilda said, "When we were here last week, patients were lying in their beds crying and moaning in pain, and no one cared."

"Our aides care. You would have to be here more than a few minutes to know what was going on."

Jessie May walked around the desk. "Mr. Silver, these people are going to visit patients here, and we will be interested in what they report back. For the next few weeks, they will be in and out. I'd advise you to get your patient care cleaned up."

Ox pulled into the visitors' lot at Night and Day. Emmett and Jessie May were right behind him. When they entered the building, the receptionist studied a paper on his desk. Ox, Emmett, and Jessie May walked past him to the elevator.

Rebecca was glad to see them, but she was obviously worried. Kitty Laker still hadn't come back. Ox made a note to pressure Starky.

Starky wasn't on the balcony so Ox knocked on her door. There was no answer. He met Emmett and Jessie May in the hallway and they decided to try later. As they were starting to pull out from the parking lot, they noticed an ambulance in the rear. They went back to investigate. Two patients were being carried into the green building.

"Where did they come from?" asked Emmett. "Rapid Creek Nursing Home."

Ox, Emmett, and Jessie May went back into the building and up to Starky's office. Ox knocked again. Emmett turned the knob and the door swung open.

Starky looked up from her desk. "Oh, what's the matter?"

"Miss Starky," said Emmett, "why are patients being transferred here from Rapid Creek? Is it because they are afraid they will be inspected?"

"We thought they would get better care here."

"In the building in back?" asked Ox.

"They needed extra care."

"All of a sudden."

"It's been done before. We have a doctor here."

"Are there more on the way?" asked Jessie May. "Remember, we will be outside watching."

Starky hesitated, looking for the right answer. "I don't make the arrangements. Mr. Bush does that. If he feels a patient needs extra care, he arranges the transfer."

"Let's get to the point," said Ox. "We know that something's wrong, and we know that you know."

"Furthermore," said Emmett, "someone's going to wind up behind bars."

"Listen, I just work here. I take orders."

"If you do something wrong because you're ordered to, you are still guilty of doing something wrong."

Starky shook her head and sat down.

"How do we get in touch with Mr. Bush?" asked Ox.

"I don't have his number."

"Your funeral," said Emmett.

Ox thought of Kitty Laker. "Is Kitty Laker still back there? If the care is so good, why is she still there?"

Starky looked sad and shook her head. "Unfortunately, Miss Laker died."

"What from? Miss Rhine said she was fine and she kept disappearing."

"Natural causes."

"I think there should be an autopsy."

"Can't. She was cremated."

"Well, we'll be in touch," said Emmett.

They were almost out of the door when Starky said, "Wait." They turned back.

"I don't have any choice. They are holding my parents and they'll kill them if I don't cooperate with them. There. I've said it. Now leave me alone."

"Where do they have them?" asked Ox.

"I wish I knew. For all I know, they've killed them already, but I don't know, so I have to do as told. If they knew I told you, I'm sure they would kill them."

CHAPTER TWENTY-SEVEN

Emmett, Jessie May, and Oster reasoned that the old police station was where Starky's parents were being held. They walked into Bush's reception area that the afternoon.

The secretary reached for the phone. "Hold it," said Oster.

He put his hand on the phone.

They tapped on the office door. No one answered. Oster took out the keys. The one to the office didn't fit. The lock had been changed.

Oster looked at the secretary. "Unlock the door."

"I'm sorry. I don't have the key."

"Look, lady, we have a search warrant. Open the door or I'll run you in."

"I'm sorry. I really don't have the key."

Oster leaned over her desk and reached for his handcuffs. Emmett tapped his shoulder. "Sarge, let's try the basement."

Oster straightened up. "Let's check the lock-up first." The lock-up was empty.

"Okay, to the basement."

In the basement, they found Bush's car in one of the garages. Oster handed Emmett the warrant. "Wait for him here."

Oster and Jessie May went back up. Oster stuck his head in the reception room. "We'll be back," he shouted.

He and Jessie May waited outside.

After a bit, Bush cracked open his door. "Who was it?"

"The police. They left."

"What the hell? How did they know I was here, Starky? Time to reinforce things." He put on his jacket and walked past his secretary "I'll be back late."

As he approached his car, there was Emmett.

"Why don't we just go back upstairs," said Emmett.

"What for?"

Emmett showed the warrant. "We'll discuss that upstairs."

They went back up. Emmett tapped on the outside door and Oster and Jessie May stepped in.

"Let's go into your office, where you weren't a few minutes ago." said Oster.

In Bush's office, Oster said, "Sit. We've been getting troubling reports about your nursing homes and the stooges you have running them."

"Our nursing homes are as good as or better than most."

"If that's so," said Oster, "God help all nursing home patients."

"We pass state inspections with flying colors."

"Then someone in the state is asleep at the switch. Either that or getting paid. If that's the case, yours won't be the only head to roll."

"I can't understand how you got a warrant to search my office. Can I see the warrant?"

"Take a good look."

He took a quick look. "Just wondering."

Oster noticed Bush only looked at the approving judge's name. "Some judges can be bought. Some can't. Good luck with that."

"We don't buy judges."

"Sit yourself in that corner while we look at everything in this room. Emmett, you go search the secretary's desk and any files out there. Jessie May, go through those files." He pointed at a two-drawer wooden file cabinet beside the desk.

Bush stood but didn't move.

"I said sit in the corner." Oster pushed the desk chair into the corner. Bush moved over and sat. "I want an attorney."

"Nobody's stopping you." Oster picked up the phone and threw it to Bush. It fell on the floor. "Pick it up."

Bush looked like an enraged bull, but he picked up the base and receiver. He held them on his lap while Jessie May and Oster looked through his files. "Go ahead. Call your fixer."

Bush just sat.

"You arrange the transfers to Night and Day from Rapid Creek?"

"I arrange transfers when they are needed."

"How do you know they're needed? How much time do you spend at Rapid Creek?"

"I don't need to be there. The administrator lets me know."

"Sarge," said Jessie May, "there are records of almost a hundred transfers to Night and Day, but they are from a number of different nursing homes. Rapid Creek is just one. There's The Clouds Nursing Home, Healthy Acres Nursing Home, Sheltering Pines Nursing Home, and Angel Bed Nursing Home. There are transfers almost every day."

"Most go right back," said Bush. "They are taken to Night and Day for extra care."

Oster was looking at papers on the desk. "Lots of figures here. Not my strong point. We'll take them with us for our accountants to go over."

"You can't take those. I'm working on them," said Bush.

"We can take what we please," said Oster.

Bush dialed a number. "The police are in my office with a search warrant. They want to take our cost figures." He listened for a few minutes. "No, they are just projections, pie in the sky. Not actual figures."

He hung up the phone. "Take them. They're a work of fiction anyhow."

CHAPTER TWENTY-EIGHT

The Nursing Home Watch Committee met and Jessie May listed the additional nursing homes associated with Night and Day and Rapid Creek. Oster attended the meeting. He had become committed to the problem.

"We don't know yet who owns these nursing homes, but we are checking it out," he said. "There's something rotten and we intend to ferret it out."

"Sergeant Oster," said Ox, "we are deeply grateful to you for your work and for allowing Emmett and Jessie May to work on this problem."

"If it's all the same to you," said Oster, "I'd like to stay for the rest of this meeting and to attend future ones until we get things straightened out."

"That would strengthen our efforts considerably. I know everyone in here will work with and cooperate with you fully. Now we have a lot of ground to cover. Not only do we have Night and Day and Rapid Creek to visit, we now have The Clouds, Healthy Acres, Sheltering Pines, and Angel Bed to watch. The word 'watch' is more appropriate than ever. Our course of action now has two major thrusts. First, we concentrate on the six we already know of. Second, we visit other nursing homes to make comparisons. Are the six worse than the rest? What comparable problems do they all share? Are there any we want to list as really good, ones we would put our own loved ones in?"

Elmer raised his hand. "I'd like to cut in here. If anyone can find one that's really good, I'd like to hear about it. The only reason I haven't moved Rebecca is I don't know where to move her. Rapid Creek was my second choice. That would have been a mistake. These places are in the phone book, but that's no recommendation. We really need a listing of good places."

"Elmer," said Ox, "you know we are all concerned about Rebecca. We will keep going over there. Hilda and Larry have already told me they want to continue with the six. We could use two more, and more wouldn't hurt."

Oster stated, "The police will focus on the six for the time being."

"Sergeant, the police presence is bound to have positive repercussions."

Ox didn't mention Starky's problem. It was imperative he "not know about it."

"There are twenty-two members of this committee. The focus on the other nursing homes will require just about everybody else. Everyone needs to coordinate. Let Angel be the central clearing office. Select the nursing home you want to call for an appointment. Let Angel know so no one else picks the same one. Duplicating later would be okay, but, initially, we want to get to as many as possible for a first visit."

Oster raised his hand. "If a nursing home says no, let me, Emmett, or Jessie May know and we will pay them an unscheduled visit."

"Excellent," said Ox. "That's perfect. It's really a stroke of good fortune that the police are involved. Let's have a short meeting every Sunday after the service."

As the meeting ended, Ox could see members pairing up. What had started out on a small scale was blossoming into a full-scale operation. He planned to visit the governor's office when more of the visits indicated the need. The Health and Human Services visit had been useless, other than to expose incompetence. He planned to follow through on that. At some point, it might be good to bring the newspapers and TV stations in on it. There was more than one way to skin a cat.

The Group met at Night and Day.

Bush reported, "There's no choice now but to either curtail the operations or at least cut it drastically. Christie has done this to us, but it's gone beyond him now with the police involved. With the police involved, it wouldn't be advisable to do anything to him. I'll still keep it in mind and watch for an opportunity to pay him back for what he's done to us."

The leader said, "Keep it in mind. He's to blame. Reduce the number of transfers and do them only between midnight and two in the morning. In the meantime, our income will take a hit. All because of Christie and that church."

CHAPTER TWENTY-NINE

Angel called Emmett and Jessie May. Jessie May answered.
"Jessie May, we have a nursing home that said no to visitors."
   "Give me the name."
   "The MacGringle Nursing Home out in the Main Line."
   "That's the high rent district. Who made the initial contact?"
   "Donald Wilson and Thomas Gardner. Two new members."
   "Okay. We'll check it out."
   Jessie May tuned to the Internet and got the address. She
called Oster.

Oster parked in front of the MacGringle Nursing Home.
Emmett and Jessie May pulled in behind him. They entered the
building. A clerk sat behind a long counter.
   Oster said, "Tell the administrator the police are here and it's
important for him to talk to us."
   "Miss Davis is the administrator." She picked up the phone
and pushed a button. "She said come on in. The office is in the
middle hall. Fourth door on the right."
   They passed a records room and a social services room and
what was probably a bathroom. Miss Davis's door was open.
She motioned for them to come in.

Oster said, "You refused to allow a church group to come in to visit your patients. Is there a good reason?"

"We prefer to call them residents. We don't want strangers wandering around. Our residents deserve privacy."

Jessie May said, "The church group simply wants to visit with residents who have no relatives or friends who can visit. Is there a problem with that?"

"Not if it's someone the resident knows. Some of our residents don't want visitors."

"You see," said Oster, "it raises questions when you refuse visitors. That group is concerned about nursing home abuse. They will be visiting all the nursing homes in the area to prevent that."

"It would be to your benefit," said Jessie May. "They are compiling a list of nursing homes to recommend to others."

"We pass state inspection, and that's recommendation enough."

"Would you mind," said Oster, "if we walked through to building?"

"Do you have a warrant?"

"If you make it necessary for us to have a search warrant, we will get one and go through every record and every file in the entire building. What will it be?"

"If all you want to do is walk through, fine, but don't disturb the residents. I'll go with you. It would be nice if we could arrange this to fit my schedule."

Oster was getting angry. "We would rather it was unscheduled. If you don't have time, you don't have to go with us. Do you accompany every visitor who comes into the building?"

"Only for inspections. We passed the state inspection, so why are you here?"

"Just to look around. Let's go."

"Do you want to start in the basement?"

"Only if you have patients down there."

"I assume then, you only want to walk through the residential areas. We can start on the west wing of the first floor."

She led the way. "This wing is all private rooms."

The hallway was well lighted. Miss Davis stopped at the nurses' station. "We have a clerk, an LPN and an aide on each wing."

They walked down the hall to the end. "It's clean," said Jessie May.

Walking back, they passed one room with the door open. A gray-haired lady was sitting by the bed reading a newspaper. She smiled and waved to them.

"Doesn't look too bad," said Emmett.

"The east wing is also private and a duplicate of this one." They looked down the hall.

Oster said, "Good enough. What's upstairs?"

"Steps or elevator?" asked Miss Davis. "Might as well take the elevator."

The second floor was similar except there was an additional aide on each wing "These are semi-private rooms—two residents in each room."

"Miss Davis," said Jessie May, "can you give us the names of any residents who seem lonely to you, people who have no one left to visit with them?

"That's what our social service group does. Also, we have a solarium on the fourth floor where we get everybody who's able and wants it for group meetings and programs. We even have a memoir writing class."

"Miss Davis," said Jessie May, "if you allowed the church group to visit anyone you wished to have visited, I'm sure they would put you on the recommended list."

"As it is, we have ninety-one percent occupancy. We don't need to be on the list."

Outside the building, Oster, Emmett, and Jessie May discussed what they saw.

Oster said, "Well, I don't think we need to worry about this place, but that woman is aggravating."

"I agree," said Emmett, "but I think there will be better fish to fry in other places."

As they got back into their cars, Jessie May said, "I wonder if nursing homes have a doctor available? That probably ought to be added to questions asked by the committee members."

"Well," said Emmett, "This was a dry run, but I guess it was worth it."

"Big difference compared to Night and Day."

CHAPTER THIRTY

Ox reflected on a comment Elmer had made earlier about the Nursing Home Watch Program: "You need to delegate some of this."

He had been taking on too much in other areas, too. His congregation was growing. He had a music director, Cynthia Neal, and a maintenance director, Ely Ferguson. He had a treasurer, Maxwell Katz, and a Sunday School and religious education director, Ellen Cullen. Angel handled the office and was taking it upon herself to recruit volunteers to help in a myriad of ways. The church was a full-time operation and then some. The Board of Trustees was busy enough with their financial and other responsibilities. He needed an advisory committee, a group to give direction to the daily goings on and to help plan for the future.

He called Elmer and asked if he would put the group together and chair it. Elmer said, "It's about time."

A little while later, Elmer called back. "Not too surprisingly, our more active members agreed right away: Hilda Danziger and Larry Pregle. Maxwell Katz said he would have been upset if I hadn't asked him. I'll dig out another two or three."

"Good. We should meet at least once a month. Hopefully, this will give me more time to work on sermons and for visitations."

Ox told Barbara about it that evening.

"That's a great idea," she said. "You ought to leave more of the nursing home business to the police and the committee. You've got the ball rolling."

"I will, except for Night and Day and Susan Starky. Somehow we've got to find her parents."

"Well, there are five other nursing homes where they may be. You can't search them, but the police can. Let Oster, Jessie May and Emmett take that on."

"Well, I might put on the detective hat once in a while."

"Yeah, I know what your 'once in a while' means."

Down at the Philadelphia police station, Jessie May sat in the squad car, waiting for Emmett. He came out of the building laughing and slipped into the car.

"What's so funny?"

"Oster."

"I never thought of him as funny."

"He found out his dentist is gay, so he's calling him the tooth fairy."

"I wouldn't want to be his dentist. Might lose a finger."

Emmett started the car. "Should we hit Night and Day?"

"Sure. No need to go in. They'll see the car in the lot. After that we can go to Bush's digs. If we sit outside his door, eventually he'll know we're there."

On the way, Emmett said, "Oster's a good cop, but he can be off the wall."

"Maybe he's been a cop too long."

"How can you be a cop too long?"

"Sometimes I feel it would be easy," said Jessie May.

"Are you tired of being a cop?"

"I guess I just want something more. Right now, what we are doing is interesting. We're stretching our minds."

"Right now, I guess we're half police and half detective."

"Maybe that's it," said Jessie May. "I want to be more than a cop. I'd like to be a detective and solve problems, not just shake my finger at jaywalkers. I want to make a real difference."

"Why don't we set our sights on becoming detectives?"

"Speaking of solving problems, what do you think is going on with that nursing home business?"

"Good question," said Emmett. "There's some kind of monkey business going on. I can't imagine what could make a nursing home a profit-making business. Maybe they're stealing gold teeth."

"They must be stealing something, but what? We've got Bush arranging transfers from five other nursing homes to Night and Day. That's really strange. Starky says it's to provide additional health care. That's a real stretch. What's going on in that back building?"

"Maybe we need to get a search warrant."

They pulled into the lot and parked in front of the entrance. In the rearview mirror, Emmett saw an ambulance leaving.

"Probably taking a patient back somewhere," said Jessie May.

"Yeah, I guess."

He turned off the engine.

"I'm sure we've been noted," said Jessie May. "Let's just sit here for a while. Maybe we'll worry somebody."

"Well, Starky has plenty to worry about, other than us. Where do you suppose her parents are?"

"In one of the other nursing homes?"

"Most likely," said Emmett.

"The question is which one?"

"Well, for all we know, they've disposed of them."

"Who's they?"

"I guess that's the question."

"That's one of the questions," said Jessie May. "Another question is 'what are they doing?'"

Susan Starky knew they were there. What was to become of her? What was to become of her parents? The police now knew about her parents, but they didn't know where they were. Her life was a waste. She had never amounted to anything. Her poor parents tried to keep her straight, but she consistently screwed up. They stuck by her even after she totally rejected them. The damn drugs messed her up. Her popularity in high school was not the kind to make a parent proud. No one would ever be proud of her. Now, she was nothing but a criminal. She owed her parents more than she could ever repay.

It would only be a matter of time before the police found out what was going on, and then she would go to jail. Well, the fact is she was already in jail—Night and Day jail. Maybe she should sneak out. Living on the street might be better. She was like the patients. No friends and maybe no relatives. She had lived on the street before . . . Then, there were her parents. She couldn't do that. They would kill them. If only she knew where they were, then she could tell the police everything. Maybe then she could do something right for a change.

CHAPTER THIRTY-ONE

Emmett and Jessie May were sitting at a large computer console in the Philadelphia Police Roundhouse.

"Here's some interesting background information about Joe Bush, a real influence peddler," said Jessie May.

"Worked for a lot of politicians."

"Including one senator who was indicted."

"Hey, here's how he got that police station. What do you know, he worked for the mayor—now ex-mayor."

"Who's he working for now?" asked Jessie May. "We've got to find who owns the nursing homes. They have to be registered."

"There it is. The Group, Incorporated. Crazy name. I'll dig further and get names."

"Their names will be in there."

"Here's a list of corporation owners."

"Let's see," said Jessie May.

"Merton J. Daniels, President and Chairman of the Board. Search for any record on him." Jessie May moved over to a different console. "Merton Daniels."

"Charles Z. Slawson," said Emmett. "Vice President. I'll check him out." They were quiet for a while as they searched through different sites.

"Well, Mr. Daniels has no criminal record," said Jessie May. "I'll see what public records reveal."

"Nothing on Slawson, so far."

"Hey, here's Daniels. He's Chairman of the Board of People's Universal Hospitals. Looks like a chain of hospitals. My Lord, hospitals and nursing homes. Is he trying to corner the market?"

"Here's Slawson. Vice President of that same chain. I'll be darned."

"That board and The Group appear to be one and the same," said Jessie May. "Now I'm confused."

"Me, too. They can't run a hospital the way they run those nursing homes."

"There's a group in Chicago that monitors all the hospitals in the country, the Joint Commission for Accreditation of Hospitals."

"I hope they're better than that bunch in Harrisburg that's supposed to monitor nursing homes," said Emmett.

"Well, they can't be any worse."

Ann Cooke had just started the evening shift at Rapid Creek. She heard shouting out in the entrance hall and ran to see what it was.

Buck Washington and Jamail Thomas were pushing Willis Taylor back and forth between them. Boyd Silver's door was shut. If he was in there, he wasn't having anything to do with it. Taylor was old and weak enough he could have a stroke. He looked ready to drop.

"Don't give me no hard time, ol' man."

Buck Washington pushed him and this time he fell. Washington looked like he was about to punt the old man's head.

Ann put all her weight behind a punch to Washington's head. Down he went. She pushed Jamail Thomas who tripped over a bench. She knew she had to put everything she had into it with these two or they would gang up on her. She hit Thomas in the stomach and he backed away. Evidently, he was too surprised and breathless to run. She slapped his face.

"That's for ganging up on an old man."

Washington was trying to get up. Ann kicked him as hard as she could in the seat. He sprawled forward. She turned back to Thomas, but he'd had enough. He turned and ran. She knew he would go out through the side entrance. The alarm had been broken for years.

Washington was getting up so she kicked him again. He sprawled and hit his head on the front door. Ann pushed the door open and Washington scooted out on all fours. He jumped to his feet just as Ann gave him a shove and he tumbled down the front steps.

It was all over in less than a minute. Ann pounded on the administrator's door and Boyd Silver opened it.

"Buck Washington and Jamail Thomas were out here beating up Mr. Taylor. I had to stop them."

"That's what the noise was?"

"Yes, and something has to be done about those two. They've also been robbing patients."

"That's quite an accusation."

"Ask Willis Taylor. He knows, too."

Willis Taylor came stumbling to the office. He leaned against the wall to keep from falling. "Those two would have killed me if it wasn't for Ann Cooke."

"Well, okay. As soon as I find replacements, I'll fire them."

"Mr. Silver, if you fired them now, it wouldn't make any difference to what gets done in this building. They don't do anything. They stopped doing any work months ago. Nobody's reported them because everybody's afraid of them."

"I'll replace them right away. I think I need a little more security here. Mr. Taylor might not be able to handle it."

"Mr. Taylor could make rounds through the whole building. A new guard could stay at the entrance. And, Mr. Silver, the side door with the busted alarm is a real security problem. They could come in that way anytime."

"I'll get Maintenance on it. Your name's Cooke, isn't it?"

"Yes."

"Well, thank you for being on top of things." He went back into his office and shut the door.

"Yeah. Sure. Thank you," said Ann.

She wondered if Washington and Thomas would be waiting for her somewhere tonight.

They would be happy to shoot her. Well, at least she would die with a clean conscience.

CHAPTER THIRTY-TWO

Ox woke up at six o'clock, but stayed in bed, thinking. His mind jumped from one subject to another. He thought of Bush and his threat. Barbara was asleep beside him. The children's bedrooms were across the hall. There was no noise from outside. He wondered why some people were so good and why others were so misguided or evil. Was it a matter of intelligence or was it exposure to different influences . . . or both? What made Starky tick? And Bush? Do misguided people really have a chance of straightening out? We are all learners. Everybody's done something dumb in their lifetimes. Do we have to get old to learn enough to be decent human beings? Why are some people twisted all of their lives? Why do some people judge others by their religion? It's a strange world. Then he thought of Miss Hahn in the Department of Human Services. It was as though she had automatic doors in her mind, closed to any new thought.

Ox got out of bed quietly so as not to awaken Barbara. He stretched and looked out of the window. Across the street, a police car was parked. He was beginning to like Oster.

Ox got dressed, had breakfast and headed for the church. He poked his head into Angel's office. "How many screams last night?"

Angel had a big grin. "Not one. Not a single one." She looked proud.

"Your dreams are getting better all the time."

Ox was still smiling when he settled behind his desk. Elmer tapped on the door and came in.

"Ox, I have a disturbing report from two committee members who visited a nursing home just north of the city in Montgomery County."

"Montgomery County? That's not one of the six."

"No, and there was no one around to stop or question them. No guard. No receptionist. They just walked in and visited with anyone they saw. First of all, the place was not clean, and the urine smell was pungent and everywhere. The patients were a sad looking lot. No one smiled. They all looked like they were waiting to die. They sat, usually in wheelchairs next to their beds. No activity. Not even a television anywhere. It was quiet. The halls were poorly lit. Aides saw them, but asked no questions. Anybody could walk in and do anything."

"I have a sinking feeling we're going to have trouble developing a list of good nursing homes."

"There's more," said Elmer. "They picked one patient and sat down to talk. He was surprised anyone would stop to talk to him. His wife wasn't living. He had no children. They were his first visitors. The shades were drawn in his room. He knew nothing of the outside world. Apparently, the nursing home staff were content to just let the patients sit. They asked the aide if they could see his patient record. The aide said there wasn't one. He got no medications. The aide said he didn't need them."

"We can multiply that poor soul by hundreds more. Neglect for money."

"They stayed through dinner time. What he got was a peanut

butter sandwich and a half-pint carton of milk. Other than that 'dinner,' no aide came in to see him. His roommate slept the whole afternoon. The aide didn't wake him up to eat. They asked the aide if there was a doctor on staff. She said they didn't need one."

Elmer shook his head, "They even walked into the kitchen. It was filthy. They saw cockroaches. They finally talked to the manager, and, get this, they were just inspected by the state. Passed with flying colors. No problem."

"We really need to talk to the governor," said Ox.

The Nursing Home Watch Committee met immediately after the Sunday service. The report Elmer made to Ox was repeated. Hilda Danziger reported on the additional visit to Rapid Creek.

"The administrator, Boyd Silver, was as unfriendly as ever. They have a new guard in front, outside Silver's office. One of the patient units was completely depressing. The patients were like mummies. They were all asleep. We went back several times. None of them seemed to move at all."

Larry Pregle added, "There was one bright spot. A Miss Cooke was the aide on the first floor, and she seemed both friendly and competent. But she was the only one."

There were two other reports, one about Healthy Acres and one about Angel Bed. They were duplicates of the Rapid Creek report with the exception of the friendly aide. Two members reported on the nursing home in Montgomery County. That created a lot of discussion.

When the meeting was over, Ox decided it was time for the trip to Harrisburg, to see the governor. He would take as many of the committee members with him as possible. He and Elmer would prepare a detailed report, including a description of the previous visit to Health and Human Services.

He still didn't know what was going on with "the six" and The Group. He wondered about Bush.

Joe Bush sat in his office. He was angry and felt violated. The police had invaded his private place. He never allowed anyone else in there. He felt watched. This was something new for him. He was on the receiving end. The police had him in their sights. He would have to find a way to get their focus elsewhere. He would have to call in some favors.

CHAPTER THIRTY-THREE

Ox came home in mid-afternoon just to get away from the office for a while. He and Barbara were sitting in the living room when they heard an argument between Billy and Martha in the kitchen.

"You're cutting yourself a bigger piece," shouted Billy. "I am not. Just be quiet," said Martha.

"You are, too. That's not in the middle."

Barbara got up and walked out to the kitchen. "What's going on?" she asked.

"You said we could have this cake, but she's cutting herself a bigger piece." Ox went out and stood in the kitchen doorway.

"Alright," said Barbara. "Martha gets to cut it in half." Billy stuck his lip out and looked betrayed.

"But Billy gets to pick first," said Barbara. Billy looked victorious.

Ox and Barbara went back out to the living room. They could hear Billy and Martha giggling.

Barbara smiled. "She's going to make sure both pieces are exactly the same. She'll be at it for a while."

Ox was constantly amazed at the wisdom of his wife. He was frequently counseling some members of his congregation about their problems. He thought of one couple who were considering divorce over the division of time between work and home life. They didn't know where to cut the cake.

Ox smiled. "Time to get back to the church."

At Rapid Creek, Ann Cooke thought about Hilda Danziger and Larry Pregle. They told her about the nursing home watch program in their church. If more people did that, there would be changes at Rapid Creek. What could she do to help with that? She knew there was something fishy about the place. Her floor was depressing, but the other floors—morgue city. Some of those patients would be carried away in ambulances and then returned. Where were they taken? She decided she would put some time in on the other floors. The aides there were downright unfriendly. She would have to do a little sneaking. Maybe at dinnertime. Sometimes the aide on two went out for coffee. Willis Taylor. Why didn't she think of him right away? He patrolled throughout the building. He was concerned about the almost dead patients on the other floors. He could let her know when the aide on two went out.

Meanwhile, Hilda Danziger and Larry Pregle were really caught up in the nursing home watch program. It might even be called an obsession. They picked another one, this time in Bucks County. It had once been affiliated with a Philadelphia hospital.

Philadelphia, Montgomery County, and Bucks County were interspersed with old mansions. Health Crest Nursing Home was located in one of them. Ghosts of the past would be haunted by the activities going on there now. Hilda and Larry stared at the monument of a building.

The beauty of the outside did not exist inside. Renovations had been extensive. It was institutional and ugly. The first impression inside was depressing. There was a table for a receptionist. Fanned around the front hall were a series of cubicles. A guard sat in one facing the entrance. There was another for an admissions clerk. A sign above it said, "Sign in and take a seat." There were two wooden chairs placed outside of it. Another cubicle was labeled "Social Service." Another was labeled "Cashier." There were two unlabeled and empty cubicles to complete the semicircle.

There were two ornate staircases curving around the two sides of the large room. The woodworks were obviously remnants of the past, now out of place. What was up those stairs made all else malapropos.

"Good grief," said Hilda.

"Ditto," said Larry.

The original walls had been knocked out and replaced with gray metal partitions creating numerous small rooms. The lights were also depressingly institutional with a single bulb hanging in each room. Each room had two beds and two bedside tables. There was a strong urine smell everywhere. Each wing had a counter blocking the entrance and serving as a nursing station.

Larry whispered to Hilda, "Fire hazard. Did the state approve this?"

They were stopped at this point by an official-looking woman in a white uniform and wearing a white nursing cap. "Can I help you?"

"We would like to visit with any of your patients who feel all alone," said Hilda.

"All of our residents have family and visitors. None are alone. We see to that."

Larry responded, "Please know we are not here to recruit members for our church. We are part of a nursing home watch program and we want to be sure yours is not one of those that neglects patients."

The nurse was obviously offended. She puffed up as though her feathers were ruffled. "That's insulting. We don't neglect our residents. We take care of them. If you have a relative or friend here to visit, you are free to do so. If not, please leave."

Hilda noticed a name tag on the nurse's uniform. "Miss Upchurch, we only want to help. You must know there are some nursing homes that have been known to neglect patients . . . residents. We are making a list of those that don't to recommend to others."

"The state inspects us every year and we always pass."

"Would you like to be on our list of preferred homes?" asked Hilda.

"We have full occupancy with a waiting list. Please leave."

"We have a group that will be meeting with the governor to discuss regulation of nursing homes," said Larry. "It might be good if we could list you as one that cooperated."

Miss Upchurch hesitated for just a moment. "I don't think so. Should I call Security?"

"No need," said Hilda. "We're sorry we bothered you."

On the way out, Larry whispered, "Those poor patients."

"Yes," said Hilda. "I shudder to think about what's going on in there."

In his church office, Ox stood and looked out the window at the busy parkway far below. "Something's got to be resolved," he said out loud. To himself, he said, *the world is full of problems. Nursing homes should be a place for rest and escape from the harshness that reality sometimes forces on us.*

CHAPTER THIRTY-FOUR

Ann Cooke caught Willis Taylor passing through her unit. "Let me know when that aide on two is out."

"Sure, but why?"

"I want to see what's going on up there."

"Not much. The patients are all asleep."

"All the time?"

"I've never heard a peep out of any of them."

"That's strange. What does the aide do?"

"I see her giving shots to some of the patients."

"When they are sleeping?"

"Seems that way."

"Let me know when she's out."

"Okay."

Ox drove Elmer over to Night and Day. When they entered, he saw Starky at her usual post. This time, she didn't retreat. She gave a hesitant wave to Ox. Ox thought she looked worried. He decided he would go see her. Maybe something happened to her parents.

He went with Elmer to visit Rebecca, but left after a few moments. He tapped on the open entrance to the balcony and stepped in. Starky actually looked relieved to see him. She struggled for words.

"How are you?"

"I'm fine, Miss Starky. I think the important question is how you are?"

"Not well. My life is a mess. I want out of this but I'm trapped."

"I'd like to help you."

"Find my parents and I will work with you to do the right thing. That would be a first in my life."

"Do you have any idea where they are?"

"No. They could have them anywhere."

The receptionist from downstairs came in. "Mr. Bush just pulled into the parking lot."

"Oh, thank you. I better get back into my office."

"I'll be in touch," said Ox. The receptionist was gone.

Ox went back into Rebecca's room. She was much brighter. She had the room to herself.

There had been no replacement for Kitty Laker.

When Ox and Elmer passed through the lobby, the receptionist nodded to them.

Willis Taylor tapped on the open patient room door where Ann Cooke had just finished changing sheets. "Aide on two is out."

Ann ran up the stairs to the second-floor unit. She went into the first room. Two patients were sound asleep. The charts at the ends of their beds had their names and nothing else. She called out their names. No response. She gently tapped on the shoulder of the first one and then the other. They might as well have been dead.

She went to the second room, and the third, and the fourth with the same lack of response. Then she went to the aide's station. She opened the medicine cabinet. There were hypodermic needles all ready, all lined up in a row. She looked in the trash can. There were empty morphine vials—lots of them.

Willis Taylor came in half running. "She's coming." Ann ran to the back stairs and down to the first floor.

Morphine. What was going on? Was that why they were all so quiet? Something else bothered her. All of them, men and women, were bald. Why?

CHAPTER THIRTY-FIVE

Ox dialed Emmett's and Jessie May's number. Emmett answered. "We've got to find Starky's parents," said Ox.

"We'd like nothing better," said Emmett. "But how?" Jessie May got on the line, too.

"I think they've got to be in one of the nursing homes, maybe together, maybe separate. If they are locked up someplace, it's logical to start in one of the six," said Ox.

"Well, we can go to each of the six and search, but we can't get a search warrant without tipping our hand," said Emmett.

"I really want to find those two," said Ox.

"Well, that idiot, Silver, said visit all you want," said Emmett. "So let's go in plain clothes. The uniform would just raise flap."

"That makes sense," said Ox, "but they have a new guard in front and the uniform might get you past. Tell him you need to see Miss Cooke. Then go to her floor. Tell her other members of the Nursing Home Watch Program had been impressed by her. Ask if you can visit on her floor."

"Makes sense," said Jessie May.

* * *

The Group was scheduled to meet at Night and Day. Bush arrived early to give Starky his usual pep talk. As usual, she collapsed under his pushing.

"I can kill them anytime I want to. Don't forget it."

"I know. I'm doing just as you tell me."

"Just for fun, I might torture them first."

"Please. I'm doing the job. I'll be the biggest bastard ever created. Don't hurt them."

"Okay. See that you are. I'm watching."

Merton Daniels conducted the meeting. "Our income has taken a hit because of the fuss started by Christie. The midnight transfers aren't enough. Rosenfeld has time on his hands. The production line has slowed down eighty percent. The needs of the hospital are now relying on legitimate sources. Mr. Bush, you have to get a handle on the process. We've got to get back to normal."

"Mr. Daniels, what if we made the transfers directly to the hospital? Could we put Rosenfeld in the hospital operating room?"

"Possible, but risky. Rosenfeld has no license and some of those damn nurses are natural whistleblowers. No, that would put the hospital at risk. Better come up with another solution. Anybody else have any ideas? Slawson, how about you? Any thoughts?"

Charles Slawson was accustomed to letting Daniels do the talking. Bush handled basic operations. He tried to come up with an intelligent idea.

"Well, I think Christie has to be stopped."

"It's a little late for that. He's got a whole damn army working now. He could disappear and we would still have the problem."

"I think we should get him anyhow. He started the mess."

"Revenge won't increase the bottom line."

* * *

Emmett and Jessie May decided to visit Starky at Night and Day before going to Rapid Creek to search for her parents. They needed a description.

"Should we call first?" asked Jessie May. "Not necessary. She's always there."

"Right."

They pulled into the lot.

"Should we drop in to see Rebecca first?" asked Emmett. "Can't hurt."

Bush was impatient with Slawson. "Mr. Daniels, I'm hesitant to make the following comment because it's not a certainty. I have some favors to call in from a few of our legislators. I'm hoping to put pressure on the police to bring about a change of focus—get them occupied with a different problem. So far, our friends haven't come up with a way to do that, but we're working on it."

"Well, even if you succeeded in that, the visits would continue."

"Yes, but then if something unfortunate happens to Christie, the police wouldn't be as integral a part of the process."

"I think if the police changed their focus and something happened to Christie, their focus would change back quickly."

Starky was standing on the balcony. She saw the police car pull into the lot. "Oh, dear God. Not now. Please."

As they entered the building, Jessie May waved to Starky. Starky waved and then motioned at the entrance of the balcony and moved in that direction.

Humphrey, the receptionist, looked absolutely startled. "Are you visiting Miss Rhine?"

"Yes," said Jessie May, "and then Miss Starky."

"She may be busy. The owners are in her office."

Jessie May understood immediately why Starky seemed upset. "Let's get upstairs in a hurry and get into Rebecca's room."

"They may see our car," Emmett said.

"That's okay. They already know we visit."

"Guess we'll meet with Starky another time."

They walked past the wheelchair patients and into Rebecca's room.

Starky was there. "I can't stay. It's too risky. The owners are here."

"The receptionist told us," said Jessie May. "We needed to get back in touch to get a description of your parents."

"Wonderful. I've got to get back to the balcony." She darted out of the room.

Just as she got back to her normal post, the office door opened and Slawson barked, "Call the limousine."

"Yes, sir."

Back in the office, door closed, Bush commented to Slawson, "An accident has to be arranged."

"That sounds like a beginning. Maybe if the leader is out of the way, the whole thing will gradually fall apart."

"What's going on?" asked Rebecca.

"The owners are meeting in Miss Starky's office," said Jessie May. "I think Miss Starky gets over-anxious when they are around."

"I was surprised to see her. She looked so upset."

"How are you doing today?" asked Emmett.

He was standing by the door so he could hear the sounds from the hallway. He figured it might be best to avoid running into the owners.

From the noise in the hallway, it became obvious that the owners were leaving. He whispered to Jessie May, "Okay, we can relax now. We can see Starky in a few minutes."

The limousine pulled up in front and The Group filed out. Starky stood behind them.

Daniels stopped and pointed at the police car. Bush stepped back into the building.

Now Starky seemed truly alarmed. Bush motioned for her to follow him to the elevator.

When they stepped out on the second floor, Starky said, "Mr. Bush . . ."

He clamped one hand over her mouth and the other around her neck. He pushed her through the balcony and into her office. He threw her to the floor.

"If I have to, I'll cut your head off and show it to your parents." Emmett heard. That was all he needed. "No visit with Starky today."

Later that afternoon, Helen and Eleanor D'Ablo walked into the Night and Day Nursing Home. They had a camera crew with them.

Humphrey looked surprised. "Can I help you?"

"We hear that patients are being abused here," said Helen. "Are you helping them? Where's the manager? We want to show these patients to the TV audience. You might want to watch the six o'clock news. Do they pay you to give warning when the authorities appear? Smile for the TV audience."

Humphrey picked up the phone. "I'll let the manager know you are here."

Starky was down in a matter of seconds. "What can I do for you?"

"We are going to take pictures of your patients for the six o'clock news."

"No," said Starky. "We can't allow the patients to be bothered. Most of them are napping. You can't impose on their privacy."

The camera crew was taking it all in. Helen turned toward the camera.

"Reports are that their napping patients are really being systematically abused. It's no wonder this woman wants to conceal what's going on behind these walls. And our incompetent police allow it to continue.

"Helen D'Ablo reporting from Night and Day Nursing Home."

CHAPTER THIRTY-SIX

Ox and Barbara attended the monthly church dinner held in the beautiful old mansion left to the church by Hosanna Lewis. Barbara left the children in the hands of a trusted babysitter.

The huge dining room table could seat twenty-six. Smaller tables seating from four to eight were scattered throughout the first floor. Some were even in the front hall. Ox, as minister, and Barbara were at the large table.

The Church always hired several caterers. It was buffet style. Everyone served themselves from the long tables in the kitchen.

These were always exceedingly friendly gatherings. Even though there was a coffee hour after church service, this offered a better way to get to know people. Sitting down for a leisurely dinner provided more opportunity for conversation and for really getting to know others. Ox noticed some tried to sit with different people each time. There were also those who tried to sit together each time. Hilda Danziger and Larry Pregle were in that group. Ox supposed these two were getting close.

Throughout the evening, Ox would overhear comments about nursing homes. Most of the comments were about horror stories. There were a few good comments, but very few. They could be summarized as the good, the bad, the ugly, the uglier, and the ugliest.

Emmett and Jessie May, in civilian clothes, sat across from Ox and Barbara. Both of them added to the comments. Nursing homes were becoming almost an obsession by more and more members of the church. He looked around at the huge dining room and could envision it as a dining hall in their own nursing and retirement home. He remembered stories from his childhood about people who lost everything and wound up in "the poor house." That term had fallen into disuse. It wasn't the same thing, but "nursing home" had some comparisons, if one had no relatives. In which case, "the nursing home" became a place to go to die. He would call the governor's office tomorrow and take as many people as possible to meet with him. Maybe the governor could apply the necessary pressure to Health and Human Services to clamp down and make some serious improvements in the nursing home industry.

Elmer leaned over Ox's shoulder. "I was walking around upstairs. Some nice bedrooms. Would certainly be nice as a retirement home for some of our older members."

Ox laughed. "I bet if we looked hard enough, we could even find a bed for Rebecca."

CHAPTER THIRTY-SEVEN

The next morning, Ox went on the Internet, found the state's website and the governor's phone number. He dialed.

"Good morning. This is the governor's office."

"Good morning. This is Reverend Oxford Christie in Philadelphia. I wonder if I could talk to the governor about a serious problem."

"Could I let him know what the problem is?"

"Of course. It's rather complicated, but it's something that requires his intervention. We have a nursing home watch program and we have been visiting patients in a number of nursing homes in Philadelphia, Montgomery County, and Bucks County. To get right to the point, we have discovered widespread nursing home abuse of patients. We would like to discuss this with the governor because it is really in epidemic proportions."

"Maybe you should talk to Health and Human Services. This is actually their responsibility. I can give you their phone number."

"Actually, we did talk to them, and, to be frank, that is what we want to discuss with him. The system is part of the problem and only he can fix it."

"Well, the governor is quite busy. He has a full schedule."

"We have put a lot of work into assessing patient care in nursing homes. It's a serious problem he should know about."

"Well, I'm looking at his schedule and any meeting would have to be several months away. Why don't I set up a meeting with the lieutenant governor? I'm sure he would be interested and he does meet with the governor daily."

Ox realized he would have to compromise. Maybe he could get to the governor through the next in command. "Fine. I'll bring a few members of the Nursing Home Watch Program with me. We will have a detailed report to give him."

"I can give you fifteen minutes Thursday at three p.m."

"I think we will need more than fifteen minutes. We have discovered massive abuse."

"I can give you thirty minutes a week from Friday, three p.m."

"Fine."

Ox figured once in, they would take the time needed. He called Elmer.

"We need to get the report for the governor finished. We have an appointment with the lieutenant governor a week from Friday at three p.m. I'm sure a number of committee members will want to go."

"Great. I'll expedite the report and get commitments from as many members as can go."

That night at home, Emmett and Jessie May discussed what they'd seen so far. "Do you have any idea about what's going on?" asked Emmett.

"I have some scary thoughts, but they are off the wall."

"Me too."

"You first."

"Okay," said Emmett. "I think they are selling body parts."

"Bingo. As far out as it sounds, there just isn't any other possibility."

"I've resisted thinking it for some time because it just sounds too preposterous."

"Yes, I know," said Jessie May. "I've heard of selling a body part once in a while, but this looks like a massive operation. Who would they be selling them to? This is a highly controlled process. And doing it on a large scale, with all those nursing homes."

"Well, the question is, what now?"

"We need to talk to Oster. He'll think we're crazy."

"It'll eventually go beyond Oster," said Emmett. "This may be state police, FBI, God knows what."

"But first we have to find Starky's parents," said Jessie May.

Night after night at the Christie dinner table, Martha asked if they could get a dog. It could be any kind of dog as long as he was fat, happy, had a wagging tail and loving eyes. She wanted a dog more than anything in the world.

Finally, after weeks of asking as soon as they sat down to eat, Barbara said, "We're not ready for a dog, *yet*. From now on, you can only ask on Mondays."

So on Tuesday dinners through Sunday dinners, Martha said, "I wish today was Monday."

The grownups had to stifle their laughs.

One night, after the kids were in bed, Barbara said to Ox, "You know what we are going to have to name the dog if we ever get one, don't you?"

"What?"

"Monday."

CHAPTER THIRTY-EIGHT

Now he was Humphrey the Receptionist, not Humphrey de la Quatro. Well, he was lucky to have the job—any job. He knew he was ugly. Why would anyone want him as a receptionist? You would think a receptionist would be anything but ugly. On top of that, he was an ex-con.

Why had they hired him? They hired his brother as an orderly. You would think they would want someone attractive to be seen by the public or to handle patients. The only answer was, they didn't want visitors. He was ugly. He wasn't stupid.

He knew they were doing something illegal. They figured he wouldn't care. He had been arrested for manslaughter, for accidentally killing his little cousin. It really was an accident, not his fault, but he was so ugly, it had been easy for the jury to find him guilty. His anger over being accused didn't help. He knew anger made him even uglier.

Now, here he was. Just by being there, he was sharing the guilt for whatever they were doing. He would be found guilty even more so because he had a record. In the beginning, he felt hard-nose Starky was the source of the evil. Now he wasn't sure. When The Group met, she stood out on the balcony, and sometimes he could tell she was upset. He was beginning to think she was being forced to do the job. They had something on her. Maybe she was a victim, like him.

He began to feel sorry for her. He went from hating her to wanting to help, but he wasn't in any position to help.

His brother told him about the transfers. As orderly, he would bring them in and then take them back out. That was something really strange. The sheer numbers were staggering. He couldn't think of anything he could do. He didn't know what was going on.

He went from hating Starky to almost liking her. When the police showed up during The Group's meeting, he was sure Starky would catch it. They blamed her for everything. He was a nobody, worthless. His life had no meaning. Maybe he could give it meaning by doing something to stop whatever was going on. Maybe he could be somebody.

"Bush is going to make it difficult for us to get to Starky," said Emmett. "How can we meet with her? We never know when he's there."

"She's always on the balcony. We visit Rebecca. She'll see us. Let her make the move. If he's there, she won't come to Rebecca's room. If he isn't, she will. She wants us to find her parents."

"We'll have to make any meeting really short. Bush could show up anytime," said Jessie May.

"Yeah," said Emmett. "He parks out front, but I wouldn't put it past him to park in the back and just drop in suddenly, surprise Starky. The man's a creep. I want to lock him up."

"Those pointed ears make him look creepy. Maybe they're in place of horns. Look for a pointed tail sticking out his pants cuff."

Starky sat in her room on the third floor. It was a little better than a prison cell, but not much. She could look out the back window, but it was dark. She couldn't see anything other than the moon or stars. She had no phone. Of course, she could go down to the office and chance it that no one would know. For a while she'd forgotten she had the police woman's card. She looked at it now. It included a home phone number. She could call her night or day. Jessie May Roberts. What would she say to her? She wanted to describe her parents. She didn't have any pictures. She had thrown away the few she had back when she had left home full of hate. Back then, she didn't know what she had. She'd thrown away her life. Maybe she could find it again.

CHAPTER THIRTY-NINE

Bishop Markham and Reverend Darner sat in the Bishop's office in Lower Manhattan.

They had just received Ox's monthly report.

"I think we made the right choice in calling Christie to the Church of the One Soul," said the bishop.

"No question about it," said Reverend Darner. "This nursing home watch program might be something we could recommend to some of our other churches."

"I think we should consider it a trial program for all of our churches in Pennsylvania." The bishop looked out of the large window at skyscrapers and clouds. "If it works well in Pennsylvania, why not the entire East Coast?"

"If nursing homes are that bad in the Philadelphia region, it stands to reason it could be the same in the rest of Pennsylvania."

"And the East Coast."

The bishop leaned back in his chair. "And the whole country. This may have national importance."

Ann Cooke tapped on Boyd Silver's door.

He opened the door. "Yes, Miss Cooke?"

"Mr. Silver, I'm sorry to bother you, but some strange things are happening on the second floor. The aide is giving shots of morphine to all the patients. It's like a morgue up there."

"Miss Cooke, I'm sure there's a good reason for whatever the aide is doing."

"Mr. Silver, please forgive me if I seem to be overstepping, but it might help if you went up there occasionally."

"Miss Cooke, some of our patients are at a point in their lives when the main thing is to relieve them of pain. That's probably the situation with the patients on the second floor. My walking through there would not change things, but feel free to walk through if it makes you feel better."

"Lord knows I have my hands full taking care of my patients. I'm one person taking care of twenty-two patients, an impossible workload, but I get it done. I just worry about the other patients. If the administrator made rounds, I think it would tell the others they need to care. I'm sorry. That's all I came to say."

Ann turned to leave. Silver reached out and held her by the arm.

"Miss Cooke, the nursing home business is complicated. It's not everybody's cup of tea. You do a good job on the first floor. Let me take care of business."

As Ann stalked out of the office, Willis Taylor saw her.

"Was old Trap Jaw giving you the business?"

"No, old Trap Jaw said I should mind my own business, and that's just what I'm going to do. He might prefer I didn't."

Ox met with the Church Advisory Committee, chaired by Elmer. They went through the usual business, starting with the treasurer's report by Maxwell Katz. He concluded with the statement, "Adding our CDs, savings, money markets, investment portfolio and cash on hand, we have a little over a million, six hundred thousand dollars. There's been talk of us setting up our own nursing and retirement center in the mansion. I think we should give it serious consideration."

"I would dearly love to see that happen," said Ox. "I keep thinking of the on-going costs. Would we eventually drain away our reserve?"

"Not if our investments continue to grow," said Katz.

"Ox," said Elmer, "Maxwell and I have gone over the costs and the projections. We've calculated the costs of administration, nursing, housekeeping, dietary, medical, and maintenance, and we can see a better than break-even situation. True, the Center will always operate marginally. The income from Medicare and Medicaid will never meet costs, if we want to do it right. We will have to always make wise investments, and who knows, we may get some donations, although we didn't factor that in."

Ox said, "The general nursing home care is so bad it should be illegal."

"Ox," said Elmer, "I want to make sure that no member of our church ever winds up in one of those torture chambers. Further, I want any member of our family of churches to be spared that fate. That's the very least we can do. We can afford it. Most other churches can't."

"I agree. Have you factored in the cost of an architect for outlining changes to the building?"

"We have two architects in the congregation who have already volunteered."

Ox laughed. "You two have really been putting things together. Okay, let's let the architects get busy. You'll need to work with them in determining the proper layout."

"Have no fear. They have both worked in hospitals."

Oster, Emmett, and Jessie May were taking a break. They sat with coffee and watched the six o'clock news. Helen D'Ablo was giving a report on police negligence, which was resulting in patient abuse in nursing homes.

"That woman has an ugly mouth," said Oster.

"Why do they even let her report the news?" wondered Emmett. "She gives the ultraconservative side," said Jessie May.

"She gives the distorted side of the news," said Oster.

"Same thing," said Jessie May.

CHAPTER FORTY

Fourteen members of the Nursing Home Watch Program in three cars headed for Harrisburg. Ox led the way into the same parking garage used for the trip to Health and Human Services. They arrived at the Lieutenant Governor's office twenty minutes ahead of schedule.

They all filed into his outer office.

The surprised secretary said, "Well, I can get some extra chairs. There's probably enough room." She buzzed her boss. "The nursing home study people are here. There are fourteen of them."

The lieutenant governor stepped out of his office. He grinned and said, "Welcome to Harrisburg. You must be really committed to this nursing home problem."

Ox introduced himself and stated the reason for their being there. "These people have given hours of their time to evaluate care given by nursing homes in the Philadelphia area and have found serious problems that appear to be more the rule than the exception."

"Won't you all come in? My secretary is getting more chairs."

When they were all finally crammed in and seated, Ox

introduced Elmer. "Mr. Weiss chairs the Nursing Home Watch Committee."

The lieutenant governor reached across the desk and shook hands with Elmer. "Call me Ed, Elmer."

"Uh, Ed, we have compiled a written report just for the record, but I'd like to give you a brief overview."

The lieutenant governor glanced at the report as Elmer continued.

"First, I'd like to say that people of Pennsylvania put their trust in nursing homes to properly care for their loved ones. We should be able to trust that good care is being given. Instead, patients are routinely neglected, resulting in serious injury. The more lucky patients are transferred to hospitals for treatment, usually in intensive care, for dehydration, diarrhea, and bed sores, all the result of continued neglect.

"Health and Human Services conducts periodic inspections, but they warn the homes by telling them when they will inspect. In all these nursing homes, massive cleanups take place prior to inspection, and then it's back to the usual neglect afterward."

Elmer gave a brief overview of each of the nursing homes the committee had visited. The lieutenant governor listened carefully. When Elmer finished, there was silence in the room for several minutes.

Finally, the lieutenant governor said, "This is kind of breathtaking. I will read this report and your comments carefully and discuss it with the governor. I will also discuss it with the people responsible for the inspection and regulation of nursing homes. You are right. We should be able to trust nursing homes to do the right thing."

He stood up. "Thank you for coming here and drawing our attention to a serious problem."

* * *

On the way back, Ox and Elmer expressed mixed feelings. "Was that a sincere response or a political one?" asked Elmer.

"Yes," said Ox.

CHAPTER FORTY-ONE

Starky knew meeting with the police would be risky. She decided to write down a description of her parents in as much detail as possible. She sat behind her desk, forsaking her usual look-out post. First, she would have to give their names. That would raise questions since her made-up name was different. She would have to give her real name—the name she should have been using anyhow.

She began. "My name is Cecelia Stallings. I was called Sissy. Susan Starky is a made-up name. My parents are Joseph and Marie Stallings. My mother is a thin, little woman with reddish brown hair, which she usually keeps tied back in a bun."

Starky began to cry. Why had she been so mean to her mother? Why had she made her mother cry? She tried to get hold of herself, got a tissue, and continued. "She has blue eyes, usually wears glasses, and the last time I saw her, had no wrinkles. She has a sweet smile, usually." Here, Starky broke down and sobbed. Her mother never hurt anyone. She was a sweet woman and didn't deserve to be hurt.

She thought she heard a noise on the balcony and shoved the paper to the back of her desk drawer. The door swung open and there stood Bush.

"Crying again, you dumb slut? You're getting what you deserve. I better not catch you talking to the police or that minister. If I do, you can kiss your parents goodbye."

Starky broke down and cried. He slammed the door and was gone. The door opened again. "You never know when I'll be here."

Starky sat as though frozen. She stared at the door, waiting for it to open again. Finally, she stood up and walked cautiously to the door and out to her usual post.

Things looked normal down below. Humphrey sat at his desk. There were no cars in the parking lot, no visitors. She stood there, her feet glued to the floor.

Her poor parents. They didn't deserve this. She did this to them. They continued to love her all through the bad years, the drug years, the street years. They never gave up on her. They didn't deserve this. They didn't deserve her. She went back into her office to continue the description.

"My father is short and stocky. He has black hair and brown eyes." She remembered him talking to her. "Sissy, you've got to get control of yourself. We love you. The drugs are hurting you."

She had spit, just to show who was boss, and then had run from the room. Her father had called after her, "Sissy." She had hated that name. Now she wanted it back.

"Oh, God, what was wrong with me?"

She put the paper back in the desk drawer and stared at the door. After a while, she picked up the phone and dialed the number she'd memorized.

"I have written a description of my parents, but let me read it to you in case I can't hand it to you."

Jessie May hung up the phone and handed Emmett the description she had written down. "Here's who we look for. Let's pay a visit to Rapid Creek."

CHAPTER FORTY-TWO

Bush was back in his office when the call came from Senator Leslie Smyth's office. "Joe, this has become a hot issue. Right now's not the time. That nursing home watch group has paid a visit to the governor's office and the lieutenant governor is putting pressure on Health and Human Services. There could be more emphasis put on it, not less."

Bush hung up the phone. Christie had really done it now. He had to be stopped. He tried to think of who else owed him a favor. Wasn't there a single politician he could trust?

Emmett and Jessie May arrived at Rapid Creek and were surprised to see a flurry of activity. Three ambulances were backed up transporting patients out.

Emmett asked one of the drivers, "Where are you taking these patients?"

"This nursing home is overcrowded and we are taking them to another."

Emmett and Jessie May looked at each of the sleeping patients. None matched the description from Starky. They went into the home and were greeted by Silver and the guard.

"We're quite busy right now. The state is inspecting tomorrow."

"I guess this is not the best time," said Emmett.

"We'll be back," said Jessie May.

When they came out, a large van pulled away from across the street. They watched it go, but there was no reason to think it was related to Rapid Creek.

Jessie May couldn't help but wonder.

Ox gave a progress report to the Unitarian Social Responsibility Committee. Eight of its members were involved in nursing home visits.

Nathan Gibbs thanked him. "I hope the trip to Harrisburg will have a positive impact on the nursing homes in Pennsylvania. If nothing else, I hope the state will stop letting them know when the inspection will take place.

Florence Ebenbach stated, "I've gotten the impression the state wants them to know so they don't have as many things wrong to report. I just think the state employees don't want to be troubled anymore than they have to be."

"Well," said Ox, "our first trip to Harrisburg would seem to confirm that, but I have to say, the lieutenant governor seemed really concerned. I guess time will tell. It wouldn't hurt if we all wrote to our senators and representatives."

"Right," said Nathan Gibbs. "Put on continuous pressure. I think we ought to beef up our program. Wouldn't it be wonderful if both groups showed up at the same nursing homes occasionally? The nursing homes need watching and they need to know the state isn't the only one watching."

Late that night, Angel parked across the street from Health Crest Nursing Home. The only light she could see was inside the front entrance. She couldn't see any people anywhere. The place looked deserted. Of course, late at night that could be expected.

It looked like an old mansion. She wondered if anyone would stop her if she went in. She sat for almost an hour. The place was dead.

Finally, she got out of the car, closing the door as quietly as possible. She walked around the building, half expecting someone to jump out of the dark and grab her. She came back out front and stood by the entrance. She could see no one inside. She walked up the steps and opened the door. She had thought it would be locked.

The door squeaked. She stood frozen. Slowly, she moved into the huge front room with its half circle of cubicles, all unmanned. Curved stairwells on both sides of the room seemed like frames.

Beneath the curved stairwell on the right, she could see what appeared to be a hallway.

There was a faint light coming from somewhere farther in. She paused and then decided she would have to see what it was.

She moved cautiously into the hallway. She felt as though the walls were closing in on her. The light was coming from a partially open doorway near the end of the hallway. She moved quietly toward the door. She heard a woman's voice. As she got closer, she could make out what the woman was saying.

"Just sign right here, Mr. Zueger. Then I'll let you get back to bed." Angel peeped around the doorframe.

"Right here, Mr. Zueger. I know you're tired and want to get back to bed. Just sign and we'll be done."

It was a nurse, dressed in her white uniform. An old man sat, half laying on a wooden desk. He looked ready to collapse.

"Just sign and we'll be done. The other patients have all signed. It's just a formality. You'll be glad you did, and you'll be able to get back to bed."

"I don't want to. I can't leave everything to this place. My wife will need it all."

"Come on, Mr. Zueger, I don't want to get angry with you. When's the last time you saw your wife?"

"She's too sick to come. She's not able to drive."

"We'll take care of your wife."

"I'm not sure I want you to take care of her."

"Face it, Mr. Zueger, you can't take care of her. Sign the paper."

"Miss Upchurch, I don't want to."

"Whether or not you want to, you have to sign it if you want to get back to bed. I can sit here all night."

"This isn't right."

"Right or wrong doesn't matter. Sign here. I'm signing, too. The other patients are signing, too. See? Here's the stack of wills, and I've signed and witnessed them all. Everybody's leaving everything to the house. After all, we're taking care of you.

"Good. Thank you, Mr. Zueger. Now, I'll wheel you back upstairs."

Angel ducked farther down the hall and prayed they would go the other way. Sure enough, Miss Upchurch emerged, wheeling Mr. Zueger out in a wheelchair, and headed out toward the front of the building. In less than a minute Angel heard the clang and then a hum of what had to be an elevator.

She walked into the small lighted room. On the small, wooden desk, there was a stack of papers, almost an inch high. She picked them up—last wills and testaments.

Angel took the stack and ran up the hall and out the front door. In her car, she felt safe. She saw Miss Upchurch come into the front room and head down the hall. Angel started her car and left.

CHAPTER FORTY-THREE

Starky got the notice from the state. They were inspecting in one week. She called Bush.

Now Bush was jumping mad. First Rapid Creek and now Night and Day. He would have to arrange more transfers . . . get the patients out of sight from the inspectors. Worst of all, he would have to let Daniels and The Group know. He knew Daniels would want an explanation. It would be considered a failure on his part. He was chief operating officer. That pest Christie had gone too far. Well, he knew that. What was he going to do about it?

Daniels would bring in temporary help from some of his hospitals to beef up the staff.

Two nursing homes, back to back, were a problem. Christie, with his trip to the governor's office, started a reaction that could be the meddlesome fool's funeral. There was no question now. An accident had to happen. Forget calling in favors from the politicians. That took too much time. A different approach was needed.

Wally Mockler, administrator of The Clouds, called Bush. "We just received notice we are being inspected in one week."

A few minutes later, Bush received a phone call from a Jack Penny in South Philadelphia. "Mr. Bush, your friend Bruno called about a certain Christie. We checked his house three times and each time there was a police car parked across the street. Someone might think you were trying to set us up."

Bush was beginning to feel snake bit. It looked like he would have to take care of Christie himself. It reminded him of his younger days when he was farther down the ladder. He had resolved never to get his hands dirty again. It could come back and bite you when someone went on an ethics binge. Maybe he would have to think of something else. There were other ways.

There had to be.

He received another call from Harrisburg. "Joe, I'll be inspecting two of your facilities shortly, and the word is there will be a few more of your facilities coming up. Anything to offer?"

"I'll make a deposit in the usual account."

Ox and Elmer visited Rebecca. Jessie May told them about Starky's phone call and the description of her parents. Humphrey, the receptionist, actually greeted them.

"Miss Rhine is lucky," he said.

They looked up, but Starky wasn't there.

On the way up the elevator, Ox said, "Well, that's a change. No Starky and the receptionist seems to have developed a personality."

"Maybe we need to get to know him."

"Strange looking guy for a receptionist."

"Yes," said Ox, "Kind of in keeping with the rest of the place."

"I'm anxious for Emmett and Jessie May to find Starky's parents. That's when things will break wide open."

Rebecca was glad to see them. "Things have improved here and I get visits every week. I never know who from. But I still miss Kitty."

Ox thought there should be some kind of activity for patients, but that was not on the agenda at Night and Day. He thought of Kitty Laker. She died with no autopsy possible. It was likely she was a victim.

When they came out of Rebecca's room, they were surprised to see two aides and a nurse wheeling the usual hall occupants into their rooms.

Elmer nodded. "Looks like our trip had some effect."

"You think?"

"Looks like they're getting ready for a repeat of the inspection they had six months ago."

"That's right. You did mention they had an inspection when you first brought Rebecca here."

Ox asked the nurse who was hurrying by, "What's going on?"

"They're having a state inspection, so they're doing what they should have been doing all along. Excuse me now. I've got patients and beds to clean up."

"Wow," said Elmer. "She sounds disgusted."

"Can't blame her. She's right. I take it she's temporary."

"Must be. Otherwise, she could jeopardize her job." The two orderlies were mopping the floor.

Elmer nudged Ox and pointed into the balcony. Bush stood where Starky usually stood. "Maybe we should wave goodbye," said Ox.

"People like him are best ignored."

"Unfortunately, you're right."

They walked out without looking up.

As Ox was pulling out of the lot, he glanced back at the green-windowed building. A sign was being placed above the entrance, "Office and Conference Area."

CHAPTER FORTY-FOUR

Angel tapped on Ox's door and then peeped in. "Ox, I have something the nursing home committee would be interested in."

She rushed in and sat in front of his desk. She plopped the pack of papers in front of him. "These are last wills and testaments signed by all the patients in Health Crest Nursing Home. They all leave everything to the nursing home, and they are forced to sign them."

She related her experience, leaving out no detail. She even quoted Miss Upchurch, showing how she browbeat Mr. Zueger.

Ox was amazed. "You went out there at night all by yourself?"

"Well, one thing led to another."

"Angel, that was dangerous. Please team up with someone before doing anything like that again."

Ox studied the papers. "My Lord, to force someone to do this is criminal. It's obviously a practice of that place. Medicare and Medicaid cover patients. If someone voluntarily leaves everything to the home, that's one thing, but to be forced . . . that's criminal."

"Ox, that Sergeant Oster scares me. I bet he would scare them."

"Well, actually, he most likely has contacts in the DA's office. That's who should check this out. Call him and tell him about it. My guess is he'll be right out here."

Ox handed the papers to Angel.

"Right," she said. She went back out to her desk.

Ox saw the phone extension button light up. He couldn't get over it. Angel was meek on the outside, but underneath, she was a force to be reckoned with.

Emmett and Jessie May were parked half a block beyond Rapid Creek. Four ambulances had pulled away in the half hour they'd been there.

"Let's follow the next one," said Emmett. "Good idea. Where the heck are they going?"

"It's obvious they want some of the patients elsewhere during the inspection," said Emmett.

Another ambulance pulled into the driveway next to the building. "That one will be leaving soon," said Jessie May.

Sure enough, in less than five minutes, it pulled out. Emmett pulled out to follow. "Six bits it's going to one of the six."

Twenty-five minutes later they were at Angel Bed Nursing Home. "Bingo," said Jessie May.

"Double bingo," said Emmett.

Sally Manierie, administrator of Angel Bed Nursing Home received a phone call from the state Health and Human Services Office.

"Miss Manierie, the state will be inspecting your facility a week from Friday." Miss Manierie called Bush's office, but he wasn't in.

"Would you tell him the state will be inspecting us a week from Friday? We are going to need some help getting ready, and we can't be receiving anymore patients. We need to transfer some."

* * *

Ann Cooke watched as patient after patient from the second floor was moved out. Soon the floor would be empty. Her own floor was left alone. None of her patients were transferred out. That was unusual. At the previous inspection, the sickest were moved, at her objection. The second floor hadn't been a morgue that time.

Willis Taylor came down her hall. She liked this old man. In his younger days, he must have been something. She was sure he was always honest. It seemed to be built in. It takes a special person to be that way through hardships imposed by social circumstances.

"Is the second floor empty now?"

"Not now."

"What do you mean?"

"They're bringing in patients with more life. Makes the unit look good."

"Lord, where are they coming from?"

"My guess would be from another of the nursing homes. Maybe from the one they are taking our lifeless ones to. Makes us look better for inspection."

"Looks like a shell game. When the inspection's over, that police couple will probably be back. I think we should spend some time with them," said Ann.

"I think you're right."

"Something's going on. This mass exodus just proves it. I can't be part of it. I want to be part of bringing it down."

"Count me in."

Boyd A. Silver sat in back of his desk. He faced the door which he kept closed. He didn't care to see the traffic in the entrance hall. At one time he had been in a more respectable position, assistant administrator in a large hospital. He'd screwed up. People the next rank down watched for any opportunity to back-stab him and take his job. It was dog eat dog and he was the big dog. Then, he'd screwed up, and they pounced. Now he had a nothing job. He'd learned to keep his mouth shut, and trust nobody.

He really didn't give a damn about the patients. They were all old and useless. Anything to justify their existence was alright with him. Some of his employees were pieces of work. That Ann Cooke was smart . . . maybe too smart.

Joe Bush would be by soon and bring new patient records and matching finance records for the transfers. He was smarter than Bush and could do his job, but he had to watch his step. From hospital administrator to half-baked nursing home adminis-trator was just a step away from nothingness. He felt like he was hanging from a cliff.

CHAPTER FORTY-FIVE

Louis Giardinelli, administrator of Healthy Acres Nursing Home, called Bush. "We just received notice that we will be inspected by the state a week from Friday."

"No! Tell them no. This is impossible. What's going on? They're ganging up on us." He slammed the phone down. "Christie. I'll kill him," he shouted. "How did he do it?"

Bush sat. He banged his head against the wall behind him. Five nursing homes. Five down and one to go. This is hell. Daniels will blame me. Why didn't I take care of Christie right from the beginning? It's my own fault. Daniels will be right. What can I do? There's no place to send all those patients. What about those hospitals of Daniels? What other choice is there?

"Christie."

The phone rang. Slowly, he picked it up. "Yes?"

"This is Carline Lambert at Sheltering Pines. We just got notification from the State. We are being inspected a week from Friday."

Merton Daniels and Charles Slawson met in Daniels' private office.

"We have a massive problem," said Daniels. "The entire

operation is at risk. Not only that, we could be exposed. This is serious. Bush has let us down. We counted on him. Now we have to count him out. And we don't have a back-up man."

"What do we do with him? If we fire him, he may talk."

"Not hardly. He's just as guilty as we are. But I have a better idea," Slawson waited for the idea, and finally said, "What?"

"He'll make a good patient."

Emmett and Jessie May decided to drop into Rapid Creek during the inspection. At least they might see it operating as it was supposed to. They were certain Starky's parents weren't there. If they had been, they would have been whisked away by one of the ambulances by now. With the pressure on, where would they be taken? Maybe they should check Bush's lock-up again.

Sergeant Oster tapped on Ox's doorframe and asked, "Reverend Christie, can I take a few moments of your time?"

"Certainly, Sergeant. Come on in."

"Reverend, I've been attending your church for several months now, and I have some questions."

"Fire away."

"Well, you guys believe we all share a kind of communal soul linked into our own individual souls, kind of networked together. Is that right?"

"Well, that's probably as good a way of putting it as any. Environment has a lot to do with it. We live in an imperfect world. There is poverty, and the experience of parents have a lot to do with the way children are brought up."

"Look, Reverend, don't get me wrong. I'd like to believe more people are good than bad, and there's the possibility that good will prevail, but I deal with people who are more like animals than human beings. In fact, apes are better than some of the people I deal with. And I deal with them repeatedly."

"I guess that's part of your environment. The best explanation I can offer is we live in a world of good versus evil. We are still trying to win that battle. One problem is that the 'good' guys fight among themselves. One group says, 'Ours is the true religion. If you don't believe as we do, you will roast in hell.'"

"So all religions are equal."

"That's really the American way . . . not that all Americans practice that."

"Well, I see many people who don't know right from wrong. Think of the people running those nursing homes. What about them? What about their souls?"

"They have a long way to go. They need to be influenced by those whose souls can provide them with an effective conscience."

"Well, until they make that trip, I'm looking forward to locking them up."

"Maybe we should make prisons into churches."

"When I was a kid," said Oster, "I thought churches were prisons."

"Can I ask you a question?"

"Shoot."

"Do you attend church because of the threat by Bush?"

"Partially."

Emmett and Jessie May pulled up in front of Rapid Creek. There were no ambulances in sight. The guard at the entrance started to say something, but seemed to think better of it.

They walked into the first-floor unit and Ann Cooke came over to them immediately. "Willis Taylor and I want to talk to you. We want to close this place down. It's a rat's nest."

"Good," said Jessie May. "You can be undercover and help us find Susan Starky's parents."

"Who is Susan Starky?"

"She's the administrator at Night and Day Nursing Home. She's on par with your Mr. Silver."

"He's not my Mr. Silver. You can have him."

"It might end that way," said Emmett. "Starky is doing the bidding of the owners because they are holding her parents. If we find her parents, she will help us crack this bunch. But if they know we are searching for her parents, they could kill them . . . and Starky."

"Well," said Ann, "they could be anywhere."

"If we give you a description, can you help us look for them here?" asked Emmett. Willis Taylor walked into the unit and joined them.

"Willis, they need our help in finding a couple, the parents of the administrator of one of the other homes."

Jessie May gave them the description while Emmett strolled back to the entrance of the unit. He wanted to be sure no one else came in. "I can tell you this," said Ann. "They aren't on this unit. If they were on the second, they've been transferred."

"What's in the basement?" asked Jessie May.

"A lot of locked doors," said Willis. "There's also a mainte-nance room and a furnace room."

"What kind of locked doors?"

"I don't know what's behind them," said Willis. "Doesn't sound like a patient area."

Boyd Silver came on the unit, and Emmett joined Jessie May. "Everything looks good on this unit," said Jessie May. "Let's go upstairs."

CHAPTER FORTY-SIX

Daniels gave the order. Dozens of ambulances began removing patients from The Clouds, Healthy Acres, Sheltering Pines, and Angel Bed nursing homes. They carried patients to emergency rooms at three of Peoples' Universal Hospitals located in Harrisburg, Summerville, and Pittsburgh. The emergency rooms in all three had been ordered to accept the patients and admit them to patient units. The order was to handle them as routine Medicare, Medicaid, or self-pay patients. The ambulances ran twenty-four hours a day for three days. All the necessary transfers were accomplished. The Peoples' Universal Hospital in Philadelphia was not included.

Bush was told to be at the administrator's office at Night and Day the day after the inspection. The Group came in and waited for him. When he was thirty minutes late, Slawson called the office. The secretary answered. Bush left the previous day, and she had not seen him since. He left no notes. His office door was locked and she didn't have a key, but she didn't consider this unusual. There were other times when he didn't come in and she didn't know where he was. He could come in at any time.

* * *

Wally Mockler, at The Clouds, reached the point of complete disgust. He had taken the job in good faith and the owners had shown nothing but total disregard for the welfare of patients.

His budget was so skimpy he couldn't hire adequate staff. He even went on patient units and cared for patients himself.

Wally had studied personnel administration in college. Then his mother died in a nursing home. He was sure she'd been neglected, and he blamed himself. He'd trusted the nursing home. At night, he would remember his mother and worry he hadn't done as much as he should have. Deep down, he realized it hadn't been his fault.

Before he accepted the job at The Clouds, he visited a number of nursing homes in the area. None of them was perfect, and most, far from it. He took the job at The Clouds thinking he could make a difference. He hadn't.

Why had all those patients been transferred in from other nursing homes and then, suddenly, transferred out? Well, he had a strong hunch why they were transferred out. It was for inspection purposes. It shouldn't be that way.

He realized he had to do something about it. The Clouds should either be vastly improved or closed. The man he had the most communication with was Joe Bush. He had his phone number. The budget needed to be increased so he could provide the kind of care people trusted him to provide. He would make it clear to Bush. Increase the budget or he would make sure the state inspector would see the worst at The Clouds. He called him.

Bush answered. "It's late. Call me tomorrow."

"We need to talk now. I'm going to be blunt. The Clouds has become a pre-morgue. These patients need and deserve better."

Wally realized Bush had hung up.

* * *

At Peoples' Universal Hospital in Harrisburg, two emergency room nurses, Pat Christopher and Leona King, were angry.

"What the hell's going on," asked Pat.

"This is insane," said Leona. "These patients seem drugged."

"Where'd they all come from?" asked Pat.

"Somewhere in Philadelphia."

"It doesn't make any sense. Why here?"

"The director said he was told to accept them."

"Who told him?"

"Don't ask me."

"We're being swamped with patients who seem drugged or abused. Do the police know about this?" asked Pat. "We've become the hospital admissions office instead of the ER."

"Well, there's nothing to do but get them processed to patient units. Let's get them out of here."

"Alright, but when we get them out of here, I'm going up to see the administrator. This doesn't make sense. It stinks."

Leona shook her head. "Best to just do as told. This isn't the first strange thing to happen in this hospital."

"What's as strange as this?"

"Hadn't you heard? Any patient in this hospital who needs a transplant gets it right away."

"All the more reason to see the administrator. Strange things can't be allowed to get in our way down here. Maybe we should contact the Joint Commission for Accreditation. I bet that would change things."

"Best to mind your own business."

CHAPTER FORTY-SEVEN

The inspections were all over. All six of the nursing homes were placed on probation and given two months to make necessary corrections. The patients were all transferred back to their usual places.

Slawson met with Starky.

"Have you heard anything from Bush?" asked Slawson.

"No, sir. It's been over a week now. Do you know where my parents are?"

"What the hell do your parents have to do with anything? Why the hell should I know where your parents are? What a dumb question."

"But Mr. Bush was holding them. He said to do as he said or he would kill them."

"Well then, that's between you and Bush. I never heard of your parents."

Susan Starky began to cry.

"I don't have time for your blubbering. Night and Day is on probation. It's your job to get it ready for inspection. Any gigs will go on your record."

There was a loud knock on the door and Oster pushed it open. He was followed in by Emmett and Jessie May.

Ox and Elmer had been alerted by Jessie May. They had waited in Rebecca's room. Now, they stood in Starky's doorway and listened.

"We have a search warrant for your entire premises, including that building in back." Oster showed the warrant and then stated, "We'll start with the building in back."

Susan was sobbing, now almost hysterically, "My parents. Bush killed them." She ran to the back window and pounded on it. "They may be down there. He killed them. It's my fault. I killed them."

She fell on the floor, tried to get up, and then fell back.

Jessie May rushed to her, knelt by her side, and held her partially up. "Susan?" She had fainted.

"She needs help."

Slawson said, "I'll get a nurse." He left the room.

He returned quickly with the aide from the second floor. They were followed a few moments later by the two orderlies.

"Get her into a bed," said Slawson.

The orderlies left for a gurney. The aide leaned against the wall and yawned.

"This might be the height of all ironies—a patient in her own nursing home," said Ox. The orderlies returned.

"Put her in with my niece, Rebecca Rhine," said Elmer. "She's lonely and can use the company."

"Good idea," said Ox. "I'll follow the orderlies to be sure they do. We'll make sure she gets visits."

"I hope she didn't have a stroke," said Jessie May. "She kind of looked like it."

"I'll call for an ambulance," said Oster. "If she had a stroke, she belongs in a hospital." He walked back down to the squad car.

Humphrey sat at his usual post, but was obviously

curious . . . the police and that Bush substitute at the same time.

Oster came back in and stopped at Humphrey's desk. "When the ambulance gets here, send them to the second floor. I told them to come to the front entrance."

"Who for?"

"Miss Starky."

"Oh, no. Have they hurt her?"

That stopped Oster in his tracks. "They?"

"That Slawson or any of the others."

"Why would they hurt her?"

Humphrey leaned forward. "Sergeant, I'm sure you already know she didn't want to be here. I don't know what they had on her, but she never left here. She lives in a room on the third floor. She ate what the patients ate, which is garbage, and she's scared to death."

"What have they got on you?"

"I needed a job and I'm too ugly for anybody else to hire me."

Oster laughed. "You don't sound like you care too much for the management of this place."

"They're crooks. There's no staff to take care of the patients. The aides are more like guards. I tried to walk on one of the units one day and was blocked, actually threatened. What are they hiding?"

"We're getting a handle on it. We may come back and ask you a few questions. You seem to have a brain in that head. When was the last time you saw Mr. Bush?"

"Been about a week. That's unusual. And Mr. Slawson is one of the officers in The Group. He usually only comes here when The Group meets. In fact, this is the first time I ever saw him when there wasn't a meeting."

"That's interesting. Thanks. You might make a good cop."

"I doubt if they'd have me. I was convicted of a crime I didn't commit, but regardless, I'm an ex-con."

"That doesn't help, but it doesn't automatically make you ineligible. We've got a few guys with question marks in their backgrounds."

Oster headed for the elevator, heard the ambulance and turned back. Two emergency techs came rushing in with a gurney. Oster motioned for them to follow him. They went up in the elevator. On the second floor, the aide pointed to Rebecca's room. In less than three minutes, they had Starky on the elevator back down. She was still unconscious. They were taking her to Temple University Hospital.

Elmer stayed with Rebecca. Oster, Emmett, Jessie May, and Ox walked around outside to the green building. Link Unger was surprised. Ox told him the police had a warrant. Unger watched them go up the stairs.

They walked up and down the hall. It was all offices. There was no sign of Dr. Rosenfeld. What could have been going on here that was off-limits? What was Rosenfeld doing in offices?

Jessie May said, "Wait a minute. This partition runs across a built-in overhead light. And the floor is tile and slopes down to a built-in drain. This was no office."

"You're right," said Emmett. "They made this into an office for the inspection. The question is what was it before?"

"What's on the other side of this wall?"

They walked around to the next room. There were the same tile floor and the light panel cut in half by the partition.

Ox studied it for a moment. "It was an operating room."

"That's why it was off-limits," said Emmett.

"What did they use it for?" asked Ox.

"My bet is they were removing organs, but I couldn't prove it," said Emmett.

"We've thought it all along," said Jessie May. "We've got to find a way to prove it."

"Starky," said Ox. "She knows."

"The D'Ablo Hour" was filled with horror stories about nursing home patients being abused while the police did nothing.

"Apparently, it's been going on for years. The owners are forcing patients to sign over their property and then they operate on them just for fun until they die.

"Helen D'Ablo signing off."

CHAPTER FORTY-EIGHT

The police pulled into Temple University Hospital's emergency parking area, red light blinking. Ox was with them. Oster was out of the car almost before it stopped.

"We're here to see Susan Starky," said Oster to the ER clerk. "She was just brought in."

"She was taken up to 305. Her husband was with her."

"Husband?"

Emmett, Jessie May, and Ox caught up with him. "Room 305. Quick."

They ran down the hallway to the elevators. Oster pushed the up button repeatedly.

Finally, the door opened. They dashed in. Oster blocked anyone else from getting on. Emmett pushed the button for three. The elevator droned up.

"Husband?" said Oster. "What husband?" They dashed out and found 305. It was empty.

Oster ran to the nurses' station. "Where is Miss Starky?"

"In her room?"

"Her room's empty."

"Her husband just wheeled her down there."

"She's not married. What did the man look like? Was she awake?"

"She had her eyes closed, but the ER said she was alright. The man said he was her husband."

"What did he look like? This is important."

"Well, older than her and kinda jowly, fat jaws."

"I remember someone like that coming out of Night and Day," said Ox. "He was a member of The Group."

"Alert your Security," said Oster. "This woman has been kidnapped."

The nurse seemed to finally realize there was a real problem. She dialed Security. "We have a problem. A patient may have been kidnapped by a man dressed in a suit. He has a funny shaped head, bigger at the bottom than at the top. Please have all exits checked. Apparently, it just happened. They may still be in the building. The patient may be asleep or unconscious. She's blonde and about thirty years old."

"Let's go down to the parking lot and then the deck," Emmett said to Jessie May. "If she's being abducted, it'll have to be by car."

Ox and Oster walked the hallways floor by floor.

"If she was unconscious, why did the ER send her up to a patient unit?" asked Ox.

"It's Friday. The Temple ER always fills up on Fridays. They probably checked her quickly and sent her up to the third floor as the back-up."

They spotted nothing that looked out of the ordinary in the hallways.

"Well, let's go see what the lovebirds found in the parking area," said Oster. They met Emmett and Jessie May by the car. They had found nothing.

Susan Starky was gone.

CHAPTER FORTY-NINE

"Abducted from under our noses," said Oster. They were driving back to Night and Day.

"I want to talk to that Slawson," said Oster.

"That man didn't strike me as being too bright," said Jessie May.

"It's obvious someone doesn't want Starky questioned," said Emmett. "Now we have to find Starky and her parents," said Jessie May.

"If they're still alive," said Oster.

They drove in silence for the rest of the way. They pulled into the parking lot at Night and Day.

"I'm going to get warrants and search every one of those nursing homes from top to bottom, and when we're done, we'll start all over again," said Oster. "They're going to wish they never saw us."

He turned to Emmett and Jessie May. "Go into that building and look at every patient. Look in every room, including the basement and the attic, if there is one. Have Slawson go with you. Any door that's locked, he either unlocks or we break it down. Look in every closet and bathroom. We're going to do the same at the other five and then start over."

Emmett and Jessie May entered the lobby.

"Tell Mr. Slawson we are here to see him," Emmett said to Humphrey.

"He left almost an hour ago," said Humphrey. "There's nobody in the office now."

"Call him and tell him we are searching the building. If there are any locked doors, he's to get here and unlock them."

"The only number I have is Mr. Bush's," said Humphrey. "Well, try it," said Emmett.

Humphrey dialed and waited. There was no answer. "Well, nothing to do but start," said Jessie May.

They began with the first floor, which had no patient rooms. It appeared to be a holdover from the time it had been a hospital. One big room enclosed with large windows looked like it might have been a gift shop. There was an empty area that looked like a cafeteria. There were rooms that had probably been offices. Nothing was locked.

In the back of the cafeteria, they walked into a kitchen. It was unoccupied but showed signs of use. They found a large pantry with wall-to-wall shelves, which were about ten percent used.

Jessie May looked at the empty space, then at the few items stored there. "No fancy food preparation here."

"Lots of peanut butter. Some diet."

"No cooks around here."

"Well, there's no food service this late in the day, if you can call it food service," said Emmett.

Back out in the hall, they found two empty bathrooms, one for men and one for women.

Both appeared unused. There were no towels, soap, or toilet paper. There was a hall closet, apparently for the storage of housekeeping items. There was a mop and a bucket, both dust collectors.

"Let's check back out front with Humphrey just in case Slawson has come in," said Jessie May.

Out front, Humphrey let them know Slawson hadn't returned.

"It's not likely," he said. "But I'll tell you what. If he appears, I'll come find you."

"Okay," said Emmett. "We'll be on the second floor for a while. We'll let you know when we go to the next floor."

They took the elevator and walked onto the balcony. They tapped on the office door and then opened it.

"How about that," said Jessie May. "Must not be much of value kept here."

They opened the desk drawers. There were three ball-point pens and an eight-and-a-half-inch tablet. That was it—nothing else.

"Did someone clean out the place?" asked Emmett.

"Either that or there never was anything here to start with."

"Starky must have had some kind of records."

It didn't take long to search every corner of the room.

"Well, now the patient rooms," said Emmett. "We need to look at everyone."

"This is going to take a while. It's going to get dark soon, and then we really can't search patient rooms. Daylight would be best and certainly not as much of an intrusion for the patients."

"Let's do as much of the second floor as we can. Then we can hit the basement," said Emmett.

"Well, there are all those patients in the hallway," said Jessie May. "We can start with them. Some of the rooms are probably empty."

"The aide should be getting them back to their beds soon. Probably the busiest time of the day."

"Maybe one of the two busy times. She had to get them into the wheelchairs to start with."

"I assume they don't sit there all night," said Emmett.

The patients were quiet. Most of them didn't seem to notice the two police gazing at them. It was as though their minds had fallen into complete disuse. Emmett and Jessie May studied each of them closely.

"Well," said Emmett, "now for the rooms."

They looked everywhere, even under the beds. Every room had a closet and a bathroom, mostly empty. Rebecca's room was the only one occupied. They stayed for a few minutes and then moved on.

"I wonder when the aide will get the patients back to their rooms," said Jessie May. "Well, I know they are usually sitting out in the hall during visiting hours," said Emmett.

The search of the empty patient rooms went on quickly.

Walking back up the hallway past the rows of sleeping patients and through the stench, Jessie May said, "This is a horrible place."

They took the elevator to the first floor and let Humphrey know they were going to the basement.

The basement hallway was poorly lighted, but at the far end there was a flickering light coming from an open door.

"Looks like the boiler room," said Emmett.

They walked down the hallway, opening doors on the way. Most of them were storage rooms and were quickly determined to hold nothing out of the ordinary.

When they got to the boiler room, they surprised a lone maintenance man. "Anything wrong?" he asked.

"Has Miss Starky been down here?" asked Emmett.

"She never comes down here."

"Has anybody else been down here today?" asked Jessie May.

"Nobody comes down here."

They checked the rest of the basement.

When they came back up, visiting hours were over and Humphrey was gone. Oster was sitting at his desk.

"We didn't get to the third floor or the attic if there is one," said Jessie May.

"I checked the back building again," said Oster. "Still no sign of the doctor. We'll keep checking it to see if they are stupid enough to remove the fake partitions and create an operating room. For now, time to call it a day."

CHAPTER FIFTY

The Nursing Home Watch Committee met after church service. The "short" meeting stretched out to an hour.

Ox asked if anyone had found a nursing home they could recommend to others.

"The closest thing would be MacGringle's," said Jessie May, "in the far west of the city, the high rent district. But the administrator was extremely guarded and went with us, almost like she was running interference. What we saw looked alright, but there was much we didn't see. For example, the kitchen."

Emmett added, "She said she didn't need our recommendation." Oster added, "She was an annoying woman."

That evoked a few laughs from the committee.

Ox asked if there were any other comments about nursing homes outside of the six.

That's what stretched the meeting out.

Fourteen nursing homes in the area had been visited by six pairs of members. One story was as bad as the next. People were put in wheelchairs while beds were being made. In three cases, it appeared the sheets were simply aired and left on. The patients sat in wheelchairs for hours.

Most homes wouldn't discuss whether or not they did background checks on the employees, some of which gave the impression you wouldn't want to cross them. In many places, staffing levels seemed to rotate with tasks such as airing or changing sheets. When the jobs were done, all but a single staff member moved on to the next floor. Many of the rooms didn't have water pitchers. Of course, with patients sitting for hours in wheelchairs, they wouldn't be accessible anyhow. Most of the hallways and rooms needed deodorizing. While many of the patients seemed aware of the visitors, they were too withdrawn to talk. Washcloths and other toilet articles were almost nonexistent. When asked if there was a doctor on staff, the answer was that they never needed one except in emergencies and that only took a phone call. In other words, they dialed for an ambulance. For the most part, staffing was sparse. What was worse, most employees seemed uncaring. The exceptions were people who appeared overworked and stressed. It was obvious these were the ones trying to do a good job. None of the homes seemed to have benefited from state inspections and none seemed the least concerned that anyone was there observing. It was as though they had been through it before with no repercussions.

Elmer commented, "These places certainly do need watching, but that's not enough. They need to be cited. They need massive behavior change. They need a complete overhaul."

"It's not just the nursing homes that need a complete overhaul," said Ox. "The state system of inspections needs a complete overhaul. I have to say, the lieutenant governor came through as far as the six are concerned. He's really sticking it to them, but he's an elected official. He's up against an entrenched host of inflexible state employees."

"Which means," said Elmer, "we will need to keep pressuring both the homes and the state. Not only that, we have to get the press involved—the real press. Not the D'Ablo sisters. We tried writing to senators and representatives, but most didn't respond and those who did gave a sales pitch of other projects they had worked on. Maybe the press can motivate them."

"You would think the press would have picked up on this already," said Oster. "We gave a press release on Merton Daniels. He's under arrest for the abduction of Susan Starky, whose real name is Cecelia Stallings. Of course, he denies it, but a witness at Temple identified him. We still haven't found Starky. The morning press gave it a few lines on page six."

Emmett said, "The six appear to have been in the business of harvesting and selling body parts. Their nursing homes appear to be body part farms. We have to prove that yet, and finding Susan Starky or Cecelia Stallings is key. It doesn't appear that any of the other nursing homes in the area are doing that, but that can't be ruled out either. After all, if they are willing to routinely neglect patients, anything is possible."

Elmer said, "The police are now working on the original six. I think the committee now should concentrate on other nursing homes. If one refuses to let you in, let Sergeant Oster, Emmett, or Jessie May know. They'll follow up and most likely gain cooperation."

CHAPTER FIFTY-ONE

Ox and Barbara were relaxing in the living room after dinner.

"Your Nursing Home Watch Program is a thing of beauty," said Barbara. "What's a nursing home watch?" asked Martha. "Do you wear it on your arm?"

"No, sweetheart," said Ox. "It's a program to watch nursing homes."

"Wouldn't you rather watch television?"

"What's a nursing home?" asked Billy.

Barbara explained. "A nursing home is a place for sick people to go to be taken care of. We are watching the people who run them to be sure they are taking good care of the patients."

"If I get another cold, can I go to a nursing home?" asked Billy.

"No," said Barbara. "We'll take care of you here. You're too young for a nursing home."

"How old do you have you be to go to a nursing home?"

"A lot older."

"That's not fair."

"Wouldn't you rather be in your own bed with Teddy if you feel bad?"

"Well, okay."

"Mommy," asked Martha, "why do they need to be watched?"

"Sometimes they forget to take care of the patients."

Martha looked confused.

"It's time for you two to go beddy-bye." The kids tiptoed up the steps.

"Well, how was your day?" asked Barbara.

"It was routine, but a nice routine. I worked on next Sunday's sermon, wrote a few letters, and shuffled some papers. I'm feeling anxious, though. I need to get back to the nursing home watch business."

"The committee's doing a pretty good job of it."

"Yes, but I'm worried about Susan Starky or Cecelia Stallings, whatever her name is. I think it's time to talk to the DA about Merton Daniels. Obviously, he knows where she is. If he tells, maybe they can bargain with a reduced sentence. I'm sure he has a lawyer. Bargaining may be the only way. At any rate, I'm going to pick up on my visits to Night and Day. Anyhow, Elmer needs a ride. I can't not do anything. How was your day?"

"Routine, but a nice routine."

At seven o'clock in the morning, Oster, Emmett, and Jessie May began their search at Night and Day. Oster rampaged through the adjunct building. Link Unger asked no questions. The building was unchanged from the previous day.

Oster went back to the front lobby. He wanted to talk with Humphrey. Humphrey spoke first. "What's going on? No boss person around. No Starky. No Bush. No Slawson."

"That's what I wanted to talk to you about," said Oster. He'd decided to confide in Humphrey and gain his cooperation as an informer. "Starky has been abducted. Bush and Slawson have both disappeared. I want to give you my phone number and ask you to call me if anyone shows up here to manage or occupy that office upstairs."

"You bet."

"What do you know about what's going on in this place?"

"Not much. My brother is an orderly, and he says they are always taking patients into the back building, and then in a few hours, they bring them back to one of the units upstairs or back into an ambulance to go somewhere else. Neither of us knows why. The patients are always asleep or knocked out. There's a doctor. Haven't seen him lately either."

"Let me know if he shows up, too. Do you know his name?"

"No. He comes in here, but not often."

Emmett and Jessie May stepped out of the elevator.

"Sarge," said Emmett, "We've searched everywhere. Found nothing."

"Okay. I guess we ought to head out. Humphrey here is going to give me a call if anything funny happens."

Cecelia Stallings woke up. She was lying on what felt like a cot. It was dark. She could see nothing. She wondered if she was blind. She had no idea where she was.

"Hello? Anybody there?"

There was no response. There was no sound. She felt weak, but she sat up, turned and put her feet on the floor. She was thirsty. Her mouth felt dry. She didn't seem to have any saliva.

What had happened? Where was she?

She thought of her parents and felt more helpless than ever. What was going to happen to her? She stood up but felt dizzy and sat back down.

She was no longer Susan Starky. That name was gone forever. She was Cecelia Stallings. She wanted to hear her father call her Sissy. She had been such a fool. She tried standing again. She used the edge of the cot to support herself, moving beside it slowly. She came to a wall in front of her. She walked, feeling the wall and then came to a corner. She followed the wall to another corner and then to another corner. She moved on to a fourth corner and then she was back to the cot. It was a small room. She followed the wall again, looking for a light switch.

There was none.

Who had put her here, and why? Was it the police? Was she in jail? She sat back down on the cot. There was nothing to do but wait . . . but for what?

CHAPTER FIFTY-TWO

Oster got a call from the squad car parked in front of the Christie residence.

"Sergeant, a car pulled up a short distance ahead of us. A man got out who matched your description of that Bush person. He looked at us, saw me looking at him and got back into the car. He's heading north. Should we pursue?"

"Is he in the black car I described?"

"Yes."

"Stay put. I'll alert the other squad car in the area to look for him."

Willis Taylor heard someone trying to get in through the side door at Rapid Creek. He looked out the window and saw Jamail Thomas and Buck Washington. He was glad the door had been fixed. They couldn't get in. He let Ann Cooke know.

"Should I let Mr. Silver know?"

"Won't do any good," said Ann. "Let's just hope they'll give up."

"We better watch all the windows on the ground floor."

Oster, Emmett, and Jessie May walked into The Clouds Nursing Home.

Oster said to the receptionist, "Tell your administrator we have a warrant to search the premises."

She dialed. "Mr. Mockler, the police are here. They say they have a warrant to search the premises."

Immediately, a door opened. A short man with black hair stepped out. "I'm Wally Mockler. How can I help you?"

Oster said, "Mr. Mockler, we have a warrant to search the entire premises. We want to go into every room, bathroom, closet, storeroom, the kitchen, maintenance areas, everywhere. Any objections?"

"None whatsoever. You are welcome. I'll go with you and unlock any doors that are locked. Will you tell me what's going on? My superior is not answering any of my phone calls, and I have problems."

"Your Mr. Bush seems to have disappeared. One of your co-administrators has been abducted. Mr. Bush's boss, Merton Daniels, has been arrested. So far, the only charge is the abduction of Susan Starky."

"Well, I've come to regret accepting this position. I've been given a budget that is totally inadequate. As a result, staffing is low, food is insufficient, and care suffers."

"How much do you know about the other nursing homes that make up the six owned by Merton Daniels and his crew?"

"Nothing, really. I met the other administrators at a meeting of the Nursing Home Society but didn't have a chance to talk to them. That was months ago."

"What are your main complaints?" Oster was beginning to like this man.

"I guess my main concern is for the welfare of the patients. We don't do enough for them. We keep records, but it's difficult with the short staffing. That's the main problem. Short staffing. Except when the state inspects, and then additional staffing is sent in. If the state saw us otherwise, we'd get closed down. And, oh yes, sometimes, patients get taken away by ambulance for no apparent reason and I never see them again."

"Do you ask anybody why?"

"Bush just says to improve care, whatever that means."

"Have you ever talked to any of the other administrators?"

"I don't know if any of them share my concerns."

Oster said, "Why don't we start on the third floor and work our way down?"

"Fine," said Mockler. "Let's take the elevator."

The top floor was clean. A few patients were in wheelchairs outside their rooms while cleaning was taking place, but most were in their beds. There was one aide and she was obviously very busy.

"Your floor looks clean," said Jessie May.

"They know I inspect every day," said Mockler.

"It shows."

They went into each patient room. They were all double rooms but quite small. Some of the patients were alert enough to notice them. A few spoke to them, apparently curious because of the police uniforms. A few seemed surprised to see anyone other than the aide.

Each bathroom was opened. There were no storage closets, only metal cabinets. "There are no phones, not even at the nurse's station," said Jessie May.

"No," said Mockler. "The budget doesn't support it. On a few occasions, I have wheeled a patient down to my office to talk to a relative or friend who couldn't get here."

Jessie May gave an approving glance at Emmett and Oster.

"The aides are all overworked in my opinion," said Mockler. "But I still push them and they understand the need. I've fired a few who didn't. We really ought to have at least two on all shifts."

There was one bedside table shared between the two patients in every room. There was a water pitcher and two glasses. The patients were only partially active at best.

They moved from the third floor to the second and then to the first. The kitchen was clean and a cook was preparing lunch for the patients. It consisted of peanut butter sandwiches and a small carton of milk.

"At least we get whole grain bread, and I pay for jelly out of my own pocket," said Mockler. "There's nothing worse than just peanut butter, too dry. The budget won't pay for anything more."

"What do you serve for breakfast?" asked Jessie May.

"The same," said Mockler. "But I buy grapes and they get a few of them."

"Who prepares the budget?" asked Oster.

"Bush, bless his heart."

"Who pays the bills?"

"Bush."

"No finance officer or accountant on staff?"

"Bush does it all."

"Now that he's disappeared, I wonder who will pay the bills," said Emmett. "If anybody," said Jessie May.

"The utility bills might not get paid," said Emmett.

"Might be a problem for all six of the nursing homes," said Jessie May.

"The D'Ablo Hour" went on and on about the police doing everything but molesting nursing home patients. "Leave those poor souls alone."

The report concluded with, "The police have been searching for a gangster named Bush, but in typical fashion, let him slip by them."

CHAPTER FIFTY-THREE

When Oster got to the Police Roundhouse, he found a note on his desk. The state police had called to let the local police know that over forty ambulances had been observed carrying patients from Philadelphia to several Peoples' Universal Hospitals in Central Pennsylvania.

Oster let Emmett and Jessie May know.

"Something's adding up," said Emmett. "That's where they are transferring patients during this siege of inspections. It stands to reason that's probably where they sell body parts and organs. Those hospitals are out of our jurisdiction. We need to coordinate with the other police departments as well as the state police and FBI."

"We need to get a search warrant to check the surgical records of the local Peoples' Universal Hospital," said Jessie May.

"I'll get it," said Oster.

"I'll bet that's where the backup staff comes from, too," said Jessie May.

As a result of the Philadelphia police calls, the attorney general assigned a task force to investigate the reasons for all the patient transfers. The police also asked them to check on organ transplants at all Peoples' Universal Hospitals in Pennsylvania.

The team found questionable processes. The donors, without exception, were no longer living. They were listed in a Universal Donor's List but not a national universal list. The term "Universal" turned out to be the Peoples' Universal Hospital's own listing The donors all appeared to have been from a number of nursing homes in the area, which in itself was a little strange. Surgical patients paid a substantial processing fee for the organs in addition to surgical and hospital charges. The entire process was questionable.

The hospitals were part of a for-profit chain owned by The Group, Incorporated. The owners were subpoenaed for questioning. The chairman had already been charged with the abduction of a key witness. Two other members had not been found.

The Chicago-based Joint Commission for Accreditation of Hospitals was notified, and an inspection team was scheduled to review processes in all of the hospitals. The state team for hospital review was also alerted.

Oster, Emmett, and Jessie May walked into Rapid Creek. The guard quickly stepped aside to let them in. Oster pushed open Silver's door.

"Mr. Silver, we have a warrant to search the premises. Any locked doors are to be unlocked. Our search begins in your office."

Boyd Silver stood up. He looked around as though to find a place to stand. "Jessie May, go through that file cabinet. Emmett, search the desk."

Silver stepped aside.

"Sarge," said Jessie May, "this file cabinet is almost empty. I don't see anything about patients or operations. There's a file listing employees, but not many of them."

"We'll take that with us."

"Sarge," said Emmett, "the desk almost appears unused, only a few pens and tablets. Other than that, zip."

"Mr. Silver, it almost appears you are just a front, an excuse for an administrator. Do you want to come with us to search the building?"

"I'll stay here. If you need me, let me know."

"Fine," said Oster. "Let's go look at the first floor. By the way, Silver, what do you do all day sitting in here?"

"I'm here to handle any problems."

"Cushy." Oster shut the door and they headed for the first-floor unit.

When the police walked into the unit, Ann Cooke immediately dropped what she was doing and greeted them.

"I'm so glad to see you," she said. "There are some strange things happening. I've been wanting to talk to you."

"That's why we're here," said Oster. "Fill us in."

"Well, for starters, patients on the second floor have all been getting morphine shots. It's like a morgue up there. My patients are mostly old and feeble, but those patients are like the living dead. And when I attempt to go up there, the aide blocks me."

"You are pretty big and look like you can handle yourself. How does she block you?"

"Well, I don't mean physically, but she demands to know why I'm there. I guess I haven't come up with a good excuse."

"Before we go up there," said Oster, "how are things on your unit? Do you mind if we conduct a complete inspection?"

"Not at all. I try to keep up with all the needs in spite of having to take care of twenty-two patients by myself. It's not easy, but I think things are in order."

Oster, Emmett, and Jessie May walked into each room together. There was a bathroom in each, but no closet. Some of the patients noticed them and seemed glad to see them. Everything was in surprisingly good order. They looked closely at every patient. There was no sign of Starky or her parents.

While they were still on the first floor, Willis Taylor appeared. He, also, looked glad to see them.

"Did you talk to Miss Cooke?" he asked.

"Yes," said Jessie May. "She's concerned about the patients on the second floor."

"It's like a morgue up there."

Oster said, "Okay, let's go take a close look."

The aide on the second floor looked startled to see them. "What do you want?"

"We have a search warrant and we are going to look in every corner," said Oster. "You have any objections?"

The aide backed away and glanced at the nurses' station. "Go ahead. I'll be at my desk."

"No, you won't," said Oster. "You'll come with us."

"But I have work to do."

"Yes, you do, with us."

All four of them walked into the first room. The two patients were asleep. Jessie May gently shook one by the shoulder. There was no response. They searched room after room with the same result.

"This is simply not normal," said Jessie May.

"Are these patients drugged?" asked Emmett. "They certainly look like it."

"They are just very sick," said the aide.

"Let's take a look at your nurses' station," said Oster.

"There's really nothing there to see."

"Good. That means it'll be a quick look."

They found Ann Cooke standing at the nurses' station. "What are you doing here?" asked the aide.

"A better question might be what are you doing here?" Ann stepped into the station and opened the medicine cabinet. "These are hypodermic needles loaded with morphine. Maybe you can explain why you are injecting all these patients."

"This is my floor. You belong on the first floor."

"That didn't answer the question," said Emmett. "Why are you injecting them?"

"Because I was ordered to and because they would be in pain if I didn't."

"Pain from what?" asked Jessie May.

"From surgery."

"They've all had surgery?"

"Yes. This is the surgical unit."

"Why does a nursing home have a surgical unit?" asked Jessie May.

"I don't know. I just do as I'm told."

"Then who told you to give all those patients injections of morphine?" asked Ann.

"What business is it of yours?" shouted the aide.

"Then I'll ask the question," said Oster. "Who did?"

"It's routine."

"Who told you? If that's your best answer, we'll take you in."

"Mr. Silver."

"Continually?"

"Yes."

"All of them?"

"How can they be surgical patients? There's no surgery done here," said Jessie May.

"I feel like I'm being ganged up on."

"You are," said Oster. "Answer."

"They are taken out by ambulance and brought back by ambulance after surgery."

"Don't they eventually recover so you can stop the injections?" asked Emmett.

The aide began to cry. "They get taken out more than once."

"Where are they taken and why repeatedly?" asked Jessie May.

"I don't know. I just know they've had surgery."

"And you never wondered why?" Jessie May looked at Oster. "Should we go look at the surgery on some of those patients?"

"Sounds reasonable. If they are so doped up, they won't object to our examining them."

"I don't think that's right," said the aide.

"Really? You are coming with us to assist," said Oster. "Miss Cooke, will you help, too?"

"Of course."

They all moved into the first patient room. Ann pulled back the covers of the first patient, an elderly woman. She pulled her gown aside and examined her and then turned her over. There was an incision on the lower left side.

"Kidney," said Ann.

"Check the other patient," said Oster. Ann did, with the same result.

"I think we just found the organ transplant farm," said Emmett.

"I would lay odds these patients are taken to Night and Day for surgery and then brought back here to wait for further harvesting," said Emmett.

Oster looked at the aide. "You aren't wearing a name tag. Shouldn't you be?"

"Nobody ever comes here but me and the ambulance men."

"What's your name?"

"Davis."

"You have a first name?"

"Phyllis."

"The DA will be wanting to talk to you. Where do you live?"

"Two blocks from here on West Oboe Avenue."

"Number?"

"Thirty-six."

"We'll check that out."

That evening, Oster had a flash of inspiration. It was time to arrange a meeting with Ann Cooke, Willis Taylor, Humphrey, and Wally Mockler. The Group would have to arrange for substitutes that day.

CHAPTER FIFTY-FOUR

Bush's residence was a huge one-story house on a fenced-in lot.

Oster stood outside, search warrant in his pocket. "We can clip the padlock. The garage door is open. Don't see any car in there. He probably figured we would be here."

"You want me to cut it?" asked Emmett. "Yeah, go ahead."

Emmett did and the three of them approached the house. The entrance was shielded by a very small porch. They tried the door and rang the bell.

After a few minutes, Oster said, "Let's walk around the house. Check windows and any other doors."

"Big place," said Jessie May.

"Check every window. I'd rather not force the door."

There were two small windows in front, one on each side of the door. They walked around and found more small windows, the kind that don't open.

"That's strange," said Jessie May.

They found a back door, also locked. They continued around and came back to the front door.

"Get the crowbar and force the door," said Oster.

Emmett went back to the car. When he came back, he deftly inserted the blade by the lock plate and pried the door open, making a mess of the frame. They walked in, Emmett carrying the crowbar.

It was quiet in the house. The front hallway opened both to the right and the left. Straight ahead was a door with a window looking out on a center plot of ground. The house was a square surrounding a private inside yard.

"Never saw anything like it," said Emmett.

The house was warm. Evidently, the air conditioner had been off for a while. Right in the middle of the enclosed yard was a pergola, octagonal in shape with a roof matching that of the house. Two steps led up to the platform and in the middle was a chair that looked like a throne.

They moved off to the right through what was obviously a living room. This connected to an oversized dining room. A large window looked out at the inside yard and the pergola. In the back was a huge kitchen running across from one side of the house to the other. It was equipped with everything that could be found in a professional kitchen. Another large window looked out into the central area.

"I think Bush liked his privacy," said Jessie May.

"It's interesting that you used the past tense," said Emmett.

On the far side of the house were two large bedrooms with massive furniture and another window looking out into the center area. The last room was another living room leading back to the front hall.

"Well," said Oster, "doesn't look like anything here."

"Yeah," said Emmett. "Let's check the center yard just for the heck of it."

They stepped outside. Bush had covered the ground with small stones, the kind found in Japanese gardens. A path led to the pergola. They stepped up onto the platform, walked around behind the chair and then walked back to the front, their footsteps sounding on the wooden floor. The chair sat on a thick fiber mat. Emmett took a seat.

"The darned thing's uncomfortable. Must be for looks."

"It's ugly," said Jessie May.

"The mat's even uglier," said Emmett.

"No accounting for some people's taste," said Jessie May.

"Let's go," said Oster.

Emmett jumped off the chair and they stepped off the pergola. It sounded like two footsteps after they got off.

"What was that?" said Emmett, "an echo?"

They stood still for a few minutes. Oster was about to head back when the sound came again. It definitely wasn't an echo of their footsteps. It was a knocking sound.

Jessie May leaned forward and knocked on the floor. A knock came in response. She knocked twice—two knocks came in response. She knocked again. This time there was a series of knocks in return.

"Somebody's under there," said Emmett.

They walked around the pergola. It was closed in on all sides. "How can anyone be under there?" asked Emmett.

"Look under the chair and ugly mat," said Oster.

Sure enough, there was a trap door. They opened it and peered in. The ground level inside was about four feet down.

There was a feeble cry. "Help."

Emmett lowered himself down. There were a man and a woman on a mat. The man was sitting up. The woman began to cry.

"Have you been under here long?"

"That Bush person kept us here," said the man.

Emmett knew before he asked. "Who are you?"

"We are Joseph and Marie Stallings," said the man. "We need water. We haven't seen anybody for days."

"Emmett, go call for an ambulance," said Oster.

CHAPTER FIFTY-FIVE

Ox thought about Cecelia Stallings. That poor girl. Where could she be? Her parents were safe now, but what about her? Merton Daniels' house, could she be there? If so, was there anyone to give her the basic necessities? If she wasn't already dead, she could be soon. Daniels was of no help. He was still denying he abducted her. What if he were told he might be charged with murder?

Where did the man live? He decided to call Emmett and Jessie May. "We don't have his address right here, but let me check," said Emmett.

In a few minutes, he called back. "He lives in Bucks County off of Route 202 near New Hope. The police already checked it, but do you think Jessie May and I should check it again?"

"I'd like to go with you."

"I'll talk to Sarge."

In a few minutes, Jessie May called. "If you have the time now, we'll pick you up."

"I'm ready when you are."

The house was more like a castle. It sat far off the road with a long driveway leading in. There was a parking area in front of the house. The driveway went on around the house, coming out on the other side into the parking area. There was yellow police tape across the wide wrap-around porch. They ducked under the tape. A patrolman stood inside the unlocked front door.

"We've already searched," he said. "I don't know what you expect to find."

"Neither do we," said Emmett. "But we are getting desperate."

An ornate staircase with carpeted steps led up to a landing where stained-glass windows let in colored light. Immediately to their left was an elevator.

"Should we start at the top?" asked Ox.

"Good idea," said Jessie May, "but I think I'd just as soon walk up."

They walked up five flights of steps to the attic, which spread across the entire structure.

It was almost empty. There were two gables on each side with double windows. "Lots of unused space," said Ox, panting from the climbing.

"At least it's well lit," said Jessie May.

They walked around the entire area looking for anything unusual. "Nothing," said Emmett.

They walked down to the fourth floor. "This is going to take a while," said Ox.

There was a wide corridor running down the middle with rooms on both sides. "Looks more like a hotel than a house," said Jessie May.

They opened the door to the first room on the left. It was a huge bedroom with a double bed and a large chest of drawers and a TV. Two doors led off to the right. Ox opened the farthest one. It was a large bathroom with a shower stall on one side. He opened it to look in. Empty.

The other door was a large walk-in closet, also empty. They opened all the drawers on the chest of drawers, empty.

"Nothing unusual here," said Emmett and he laughed. "Just an everyday bedroom with a private bathroom."

They walked down the hallway to the next room on the left. It, too, had a double bed, chest of drawers, TV, bathroom, and a walk-in closet.

There were four such rooms on each side of the hallway. They checked all eight very carefully, even looking under the beds.

"Well, down to the third floor," said Emmett.

They were amazed. It was a duplicate of the fourth floor in every way.

"These rooms look less like guest rooms and more like permanent residencies with those large walk-in closets," said Jessie May.

"You could almost have a nursing home here," said Ox, "except it might be too superior to any that exist in the real world."

They walked down to the second floor. Again, there were four doors on each side. The first room on the left appeared to be in use. The walk-in closet was filled with suits. The drawers were stuffed with clothes: socks, shirts, underwear, pajamas. The second room, however, showed no sign of use. They proceeded through the rest.

"That's strange," said Ox. "Twenty-four rooms and only one in use. That was obviously Daniels' room."

On the first floor, there was a large living room. At the far end was a large mounted flat-screen TV, about five feet by five feet.

"I've never seen anything like that," said Emmett.

There were six leather lounge recliner chairs facing it. At the other end was the longest leather couch they'd ever seen. Along the inside wall were paintings. It looked like an art gallery. There were four large windows opening onto the porch. Tables took up the space between the windows. The rug looked like a wall-to-wall oriental.

"Good grief," said Jessie May.

Next was a library with wall-to-wall shelves filled with books, most of them apparently leather bound.

"Daniels likes leather," said Emmett.

"I wonder if they are for looks or if anyone ever read them," said Jessie May.

Then came a huge kitchen running across the entire rear of the house. It was equipped with everything imaginable, including a large walk-in refrigerator. Implements of every description hung from the ceiling over a long chopping-block table. There was a double stainless steel sink. There were two gas stoves, a large microwave oven and a table crowded with devices: a large toaster, a blender, a bread machine, a coffee maker.

On the center of the inside wall there was a small door. Emmett opened it. Stairs led down.

"I guess there's a full basement as well," said Emmett.

"Does this guy live alone?" asked Ox. "How can one person use all this equipment?"

"Or all this space?" asked Jessie May. "I imagine he has, or had, a staff of cooks and cleaners to do everything for him."

"They're probably all in limbo now that he's incarcerated," said Emmett. They crossed to the other end of the kitchen to a sliding glass door that led into a dining room. Above a large feathered oak table hung an ornamental chandelier. Along the inside wall was a long buffet.

Around the table were sixteen leather-back chairs, and in the middle of the table was a large lazy Susan. One person could sit at the table and turn the lazy Susan, thus reaching everything.

"Ostentatious," said Ox.

"Well, now down to the basement," said Emmett. "I wonder what marvels he has down there."

They stared down the basement steps. It was pitch dark. "No windows down there," said Ox.

There was a light switch to the right just inside the door. Emmett switched it on and bright light flooded up the steps. They walked down. A huge furnace sat in the middle of the basement. Next to it sat a large water tank. They stood at the foot of the steps. There were what looked like worktables along one wall. A workbench sat at the far end with tools hanging from hooks overhead. There were shelves filled with odds and ends, cans of paint and cleaning supplies. The shelves near the steps were filled with canned goods. There was a large chest freezer. In one corner, partially closed in, was what had once been a coal bin. They walked around the basement.

"Look for anything unusual," said Ox.

"Sure," said Emmett, "as if the whole place isn't unusual."

In the far corner was what appeared to be a walk-in safe, complete with a tumbler lock. It was locked tight.

"Okay," said Ox. "We either have to get the combination or force this open."

"I'll go out and call Oster," said Jessie May. "They should have opened this with the first search and left it open. He should be able to get the combination from Daniels."

Ox and Emmett milled around in the basement for the next fifteen minutes. Jessie May finally came back down.

"Oster says Daniels claims he forgot the combination, that it hasn't been opened in years. A team is on the way to crack it open."

Oster called the DA's office. There was a particular assistant DA he liked, Hayley Buchannan. He set up an appointment with her. Late that afternoon, he walked into her office.

"Buchannan, take a look at these last wills and testaments. I'll tell you they are all from a nursing home and all the signatures were forced."

Miss Buchannan studied them. "Where did you get them, Oster?"

"From a member of a nursing home watch program."

Miss Buchannan didn't ask how the member got them. "These are for a nursing home outside my jurisdiction, but I can pass them on to my counterpart in Montgomery County."

"You think this Miss Upchurch can be put out of business?"

"No doubt about it, and the nursing home could lose its license. If these really were coerced, there could be some jail time."

"Can you keep me posted?"

"Will do, Oster. Keep behaving yourself."

"You, too, Buchannan, and thanks."

CHAPTER FIFTY-SIX

Cecelia Stalling was too weak to walk around the walls anymore. She must have done it a hundred times. There was no door. She was sealed in. She must be buried. This was a burial vault. Still, every now and then, she thought she heard a noise. Each time she had yelled as loud as she could. Now, she was too weak to yell. Her throat was dry. The last time she called, all she managed was a rasping noise.

She lay back down on the cot, and now she didn't want to get up. She just wanted to lay there and dream.

She dreamed she was back home, only this time she was happy. Her parents were happy.

They all loved each other. Everything was wonderful.

She relaxed. She had never felt so happy in her life. Everything was so peaceful. She had never felt so peaceful. She never wanted to open her eyes again. So peaceful.

CHAPTER FIFTY-SEVEN

Emmett was waiting outside when the squad car pulled in. A short old man got out. He was lugging an extra-large toolbox.

"This way," said Emmett.

The man followed him into the basement to the safe and put down the toolbox with a bang. He stared at the safe, then spun the tumbler and listened to the clicking. Finally, he reached into his bag and removed a drill with a long narrow bit. He began drilling and continued drilling for over twenty minutes, stopping several times to listen to the clicking. He turned the dial. Then he drilled again. After what seemed like forever, he withdrew the bit and replaced it with a larger one.

"Difficult one," he said.

He started drilling in the same hole, making it larger. After another fifteen minutes, he withdrew the bit, listened to the lock, and placed the bit in a carrying case. He pulled out a small tube, inserted it and said, "You might want to stand back."

"Is that an explosive?" asked Ox. "There might be a girl in there."

"If so, she's probably dead. This safe is airtight. No air can get in. Anyhow, this will result in more damage outside than in."

Ox noticed a fuse sticking out of the end of the tube. The man lit it and stepped back.

The explosion actually sounded muffled. The door swung open. The man shined a light in. A few wisps of smoke were the only indications of the explosion.

The safe was lined on both sides with trays. Ox was the first in, followed by Jessie May. "Well, obviously, Cecelia Stallings isn't here," said Ox.

They stood around just staring at the trays. Finally, Ox opened a few just to see if they were real. He glanced at various papers, bank statements, a last will and testament, old letters, the deed to the property. He shrugged. "Might be worth looking at later. What now?"

They walked back upstairs and onto the porch. "Let's walk around the porch," said Jessie May. "Yeah," said Emmett.

It was a wide porch. The flooring was mahogany brown. The railing consisted of balustrades with varying shapes. The handrail along the top was wide enough to sit on. Coming around to the back, they were surprised to see a long garage. It had seven overhead doors.

"Well," said Ox, "the search isn't over yet."

Side steps led down and they were quickly opening a side door to the long structure. It was empty.

"Is this whole place a front or what?" asked Emmett. "All this unused space."

"Just one bedroom so far," said Jessie May.

"And the safe," said Ox. "Although there were some papers in there."

They walked the length of the multiple car garage. Stairways at both ends led up. They mounted the stairs and entered a long attic, also empty.

"Rats," said Emmett.

"Should we check to see if there's anything under the porch?" asked Jessie May.

"I guess we should," said Ox, "but it's only two steps off ground level."

They walked around the house, peeking between shrubs at empty ground under the porch.

Once again, they came up empty.

"Where could she be?" said Jessie May.

"I wonder if he has a summer house or a cabin somewhere," said Ox.

"Good question," said Emmett. "If so, it should be registered." He headed for the squad car to make a call.

"Try anything owned by The Group," called Ox.

CHAPTER FIFTY-EIGHT

Ann Cooke called Oster. "Sergeant, the locked rooms in the basement were not opened when you were over here."

"We'll be over there tomorrow. In the meantime, can you and Mr. Taylor keep an eye on things?"

"We'll do our best."

Emmett called Oster to let him know they had come up dry in the search for Susan Starky/Cecelia Stallings.

Back at the church, Ox called the DA, Cynthia Williamson. "Miss Williamson, Mr. Daniels knows where Cecelia Stallings is. She's stashed somewhere and is probably dependent on Daniels for food and water. Unless he talks soon, she may die. Is it possible to make a deal with him?"

"We'll talk to his attorney. If he lets her die, he could face a murder charge."

Oster put out an all-points for Joe Bush, giving a description of his car and the license number. The all-points included all of Pennsylvania, New Jersey, Delaware, and New York.

* * *

Ox described Merton Daniels' mansion to Barbara. "If he doesn't talk soon, Cecelia Stallings may die, assuming she isn't already dead."

"Would Bush be likely to know where Daniels would stash her?"

"Possibly, but no one knows where he is."

"Who's running Night and Day now?"

"Good question. I'll call Elmer. It's time for a visit to Rebecca."

"Maybe I should go with you."

"Not this time. I'm going to walk through the whole place."

"Maybe you should take Emmett and Jessie May with you."

"They've got plenty to do looking for Stallings. Maybe some members of the committee."

"Hilda and Larry."

"I'll call them."

At People's Universal Hospital in Harrisburg, Nurse Pat Christopher walked into the administrator's outer office. "I want to see Miss Hillman," she said to the secretary.

"Her schedule is full today. I'll see if I can set up an appointment for you. Can you tell me why you want to see her?"

"It's a personal matter."

"Well, I'll let you know."

CHAPTER FIFTY-NINE

Humphrey stood up when Ox, Elmer, Hilda, and Larry came in. "Two members of The Group are in the office."

"Daniels and Bush?" asked Ox.

"No. I don't know their names, but I remember them coming in with the rest."

"We'll drop in on them after we visit Rebecca."

"She has two visitors, now."

They found Florence Ebenbach and Adelle Mitchell chatting with Rebecca. "Thank goodness," said Elmer. "We've had our hands full checking all those other nursing homes."

"How do the others compare with here?" asked Rebecca.

"Depends on where you look," said Hilda.

"I'd say in all of them, your room is the best," said Larry.

"I don't know if I should be happy or depressed," said Rebecca.

"Does the aide keep your room on her schedule?" asked Larry.

"Actually, more often than ever."

"She's been in here twice since we came in," said Adelle. "The visiting has been effective," said Hilda.

"At least in this room," said Ox.

"Should we drop in on the big wheels?" asked Larry.

"Are some of the owners here?" asked Adelle.

"Humphrey says two of them are in the office," said Larry.

"Why don't we all go?" asked Florence.

"Great," said Ox. "That should capture their attention. Then we can all tour the building."

Ox led the way. He opened the door without knocking. He recognized the two members of The Group. In addition, there was the big doctor, sitting by the window. He looked annoyed, as usual.

"Who are all of you?" asked one of the men. He stood up behind the desk. Ox noticed the flash of diamond cufflinks and the diamond tie tack. He looked at the other man and noticed the same.

"I was just going to ask you the same," said Ox. "I'm Oxford Christie. This is Elmer Weiss. His niece is a patient here. This is Larry Pregle, Hilda Danziger, Florence Ebenbach, and Adelle Mitchell. We are members of two different nursing home watch programs. Are you members of The Group?"

"Two of us are."

"We know Merton Daniels, Charles Slawson, and Joe Bush. We don't know you. We do recognize the doctor."

"What can we do for you?"

"Is there some reason for you not giving us your names?" asked Adelle. Ox was both surprised and amused.

"Do you need to know?"

"It would just be the polite thing to do."

The man looked exasperated. "I'm Thomas Brame. This is Donald Suggs."

"Do you have any idea where Mr. Daniels took Susan Starky?" asked Ox.

"I don't know that he took her anywhere."

"Could she be in this building or the back building?"

"Extremely unlikely."

"Well, we'll walk around just to be sure." Mr. Brame shrugged and sat down.

Ox led the way out. Elmer decided to spend more time with Rebecca.

It took thirty minutes to go through the building. The maintenance man escorted them through every inch of the basement.

They went out the rear door to the back building.

"What was going on in this building is the reason we need Starky-Stallings," said Ox. Link Unger seemed glad to see all of them. "Nothing been going on up there for days," he said.

"Have you seen Starky?" asked Ox.

"Not for days."

"Has the doctor been back here?"

"Him neither."

"Has anybody been here?"

"Nobody."

"Well, let's take a look," said Ox.

Another thirty-plus minutes and they trooped back into the front building and Rebecca's room.

The aide actually lugged in additional chairs.

"I think Rebecca's safe here," Ox whispered to Elmer.

"For the time being," said Elmer.

Ox kept thinking about the diamonds. They seemed beyond the ordinary for anyone in the nursing home business.

CHAPTER SIXTY

Ox decided he would visit Mr. and Mrs. Stallings. They were in a medical unit and the hospital had the presence of mind to put them together in a semi-private room.

"Mr. and Mrs. Stallings, I'm Oxford Christie. My church has a nursing home watch program. I met your daughter, Cecelia, at Night and Day Nursing Home. I'm sorry to have to tell you, she was the administrator and was doing what she was told to do under the threat that if she didn't, they would kill you."

Marie Stallings began to cry. "She should have just let them do it."

"It's all right, sweetheart, she was doing what she had to do."

"That's right," said Ox. "You can be proud of her. She had no choice. She made it clear to us she wanted to work with the police to put an end to some questionable practices. But now she's been abducted by the CEO of The Group that owns the nursing home. We are trying to find her. We found you in that cubicle under Joe Bush's pergola and we will find her. Do you know how long you were under that pergola?"

"I guess we just lost track of time," said Joseph Stallings. "They kept moving us around."

"You weren't always under that place?"

"At one time, I think we were in a hospital, or it could have been a nursing home. A nurse or something kept giving us shots of something. I would be just about awake when here she came again."

"I guess you have no idea what nursing home that could have been."

"No. It was just a room as far as I could tell."

"Can you describe the nurse?"

"To be honest, I couldn't see too well. It was like I was in a fog."

"Me too," said Marie Stallings. "But we were in one room where you could hear heavy machinery or something. There was no light, but we could see light through the crack under the door. A man came in to feed us once a day."

"What did he look like?"

"He always looked angry. He was kinda tall and had a crew type haircut. Not thin, but not heavy."

Ox thought that could be Boyd Silver, but it was certainly vague.

"What are you going to do to Cecelia when you find her?" asked Joseph Stallings.

"She wanted to work with us to bring charges against the owners of the nursing home. We think they were breaking the law in a number of areas, but your daughter couldn't help us for fear of them hurting you."

Marie Stallings began crying again.

"Your daughter loves you very much. Now, we are concerned about her well-being. Right at this moment, there is a search for her going on. The fact that you might have been held in one of their nursing homes gives me hope. They might have stashed her in one, too. I'll let the police know that."

"Will you let us know when you find her?" asked Joseph Stallings.

"Oh, you'll know immediately, and she will be relieved to know you are alright. She's been worried about you."

Marie Stallings regained her composure. "That place they had us under that, what did you call it? Pergola? Was like being in a pit. It was dark and we couldn't find a door. It was like being buried alive, except for the trap door in the ceiling."

As Ox drove home, he kept thinking about Marie Stallings' comment: "We couldn't find a door. It was like being buried alive, except for the trap door in the ceiling."

He wanted to go back to Daniels' mansion and study the flooring in the basement again.

CHAPTER SIXTY-ONE

Oster took Emmett and Jessie May with him to Rapid Creek. He slammed open the door to Silver's office.

"Get your butt off that chair. Grab your keys. You're going with us to the basement and unlock every door. Now."

Silver opened a desk drawer and took out a ring of keys. Without saying a word, he followed the police. In the basement, he unlocked the first door, and as Oster, Emmett, and Jessie May entered, he moved on to the next door, unlocking it. By the time the police had come out of the first room, he had all the other doors open. He stood at the end of the hallway by the door to the furnace room and waited.

The first room was used for storage of lawn equipment: a variety of rakes, throw cloths, empty gasoline cans, extra spark plugs, two large mowers, cycles, battery-operated trimmers, and hedge clippers.

"A lot of equipment for so little yard space," said Emmett.

"Next room," said Oster.

One room was used as a workshop, including buzz saws, benches with vices, a wall filled with tools on hooks, wrenches, hammers, screwdrivers, pliers, knives, and bits. The room reeked with the heavy smell of oil.

Another was a paint shop. There was apparently no staff to maintain it. Everything looked new. The walls were lined with shelves filled with cans of paint and linseed oil. In a corner was a stack of drop cloths. Hanging on part of another wall was a variety of paintbrushes.

It took less than a half hour to go through all of the rooms. "Well," said Oster, "back to square one."

They left the basement and Silver jangling his keys.

Ox realized he couldn't get into Daniels' mansion without the police. It was roped off with police tape. He called Emmett and Jessie May and explained the room without doors idea. They agreed to meet there.

Forty minutes later, they stood in the basement of Daniels' house. Although the basement was lighted, Emmett had a flashlight. He played it on the floor, looking for any cracks. Inch by inch, they covered the entire floor.

"Look in the safe," said Ox.

They stood outside the safe, and Emmett played the light slowly across the floor. They hadn't noticed before that the floor in the safe was smooth, almost like a plastic, not like the cement floor in the basement.

"That's strange," said Ox.

"Don't see anything that looks like a trap door," said Jessie May.

Ox looked at the wall full of pullout trays. He grabbed the frame and pulled. It swung out like a door, exposing an additional section of flooring. Sure enough, there was a set-in handle for a trap door.

"We found her," said Emmett.

He grabbed the handle and pulled up. It opened easily. He shined the light in, Ox looking over his shoulder. There was an empty cot, but no Cecelia Stallings.

"Rats," said Emmett. "Now what."

"The garage," said Ox. "We've got a lot of floor to cover."

"Including nursing home basements," said Jessie May.

CHAPTER SIXTY-TWO

The Nursing Home Watch Committee met with another disturbing report. At one nursing home, there was a large room for patients with no known relatives. It contained sixteen cribs in which patients were kept twenty-four hours a day. The cribs were so close together, it was difficult to get close to the patients. Some of them were crying and calling for help. It was clear evidence that the state was not doing anything near adequate inspections.

At Peoples' Universal Hospital in Harrisburg, Pat Christopher made another trip to the administrator's office.

"You still haven't set up an appointment for me," she said to the secretary.

"Miss Hillman is very busy. If you have a personal problem, why not go to the Personnel Department. They have counselors there."

"My personal problem has to do with operating matters. I understand the state police were interested in the flood of nursing home patients in our emergency room. Tell Miss Hillman so are the ER employees."

"I'll tell her."

"Tell her I'd like to talk to her."

"I'll let you know."

* * *

Oster was meeting with Emmett and Jessie May.

"Checking the flooring in all six nursing home basements is going to take forever. Christie keeps coming up with more leads to check out. I'm beginning to think we should make him an honorary policeman. He might have missed his calling."

"I think Christie would like that," said Jessie May.

"Sarge," said Emmett, "Maybe that Dr. Rosenfeld can give us a clue or two. The creep might know where Starky is. He's got lots to lose if she testifies to his illegal surgeries."

"All the more reason he'll clam up."

"Maybe we can scare him into cooperating. If she dies, he has aided and abetted a murder."

"That's what he's been doing all along."

"Well then, let's scare him," said Emmett.

"If nothing else, we could search his house," said Jessie May.

Oster had no problem getting a warrant. All he had to do was mention nursing homes. "If only the state was as concerned as we are," he said.

"If only they were half as concerned," said Jessie May.

Rosenfeld lived in a luxury apartment near Center City. He looked shocked to see the police.

"I was just going out for dinner." He stepped back to let them in.

It was a typical bachelor apartment—bare walls except for his medical school diploma.

The search took every bit of ten minutes.

Oster fixed his gaze on Rosenfeld. "Where is Susan Starky?"

"How would I know?"

"You don't want her to be found. She'll implicate you. But

that's going to happen anyhow. We know your medical license was voided. Where is she?"

"I don't know."

"If she dies, you'll be an accessory to murder. All your other problems will pale to insignificance. You can practice medicine in the prison shower room."

"Look I don't know where Daniels took her. He abducted her. He knows where she is."

"You've built up a nice bank account. Won't do you any good in prison. You might want to cooperate and see if the state can do anything for you."

"I have nothing to hide."

"Really? How many kidneys have you removed?"

"I only do what's good for the patient. First do no harm."

"Oh sure. First do what's good for your bankroll. I'm going to do first what's good for the public and make sure you go to prison where you can first do no harm, jackass. And if Susan Starky is dead when we find her, we'll see if we can schedule a nice chair to stop you from doing any harm."

"Wow," Jessie May whispered to Emmett.

"Listen. I only did what I was told to do."

"Yeah, yeah, sure. Just be aware, if Starky dies, you go up for murder."

Outside, Oster said, "He only did what he was told to do and got paid for it like any hit man. Maybe we can arrange a special chair for him for all the patients he killed."

"Where's the press?" said Jessie May. "There's only those sicko D'Ablo sisters being a nuisance. You released a report to the press some time ago."

"Guess I need to kick somebody," said Oster.

CHAPTER SIXTY-THREE

Ox and Elmer visited Rebecca and now were on the way back.

"I'll be glad when we can move Rebecca from Night and Day and into the One Soul House," said Elmer.

"How's the renovation coming?"

"Moving quickly. I give it another month, and we'll be ready."

"I hope you are not being too optimistic."

"No. Our architects did a rush job and we've got the construction inside almost completed. The kitchen is the last major project and it's almost done. We found a dietitian to oversee the operation of the kitchen. We are still looking for an administrator."

"Why don't you do that?"

"No, we want somebody with positive experience. I might do it until then, but I'm too old to really take it on with all the complexities."

"Might take a while to find someone, given the state of the art in nursing homes these days."

"We might have a lead on a good nurse with administrative experience, two talents rolled into one."

"Sounds good. Rebecca might be our first occupant."

"That's my goal," said Elmer.

As they drew closer to the church, Elmer said, "Want to come over and take a look now?"

"I'd like to, but I can't. I've got to spark the search for Cecelia Stallings. If we don't find her, the case against The Group will be more difficult. She's the key witness. I'm worried about her."

"I have to admit, my opinion of her has changed a hundred and eighty degrees. We didn't know what she was going through."

Ox dropped Elmer off at the mansion and went to the church. He hoped Oster, Emmett, and Jessie May were searching for Stallings. He had to adjust his thinking from Starky to Stallings. He feared she was dead or near death.

He called Emmett and Jessie May. "Has Daniels coughed up her location?"

"Not yet," said Jessie May. "I understand they're interrogating him now."

"If only we could give him truth serum."

"We know she's not at Night and Day. We're going to Rapid Creek. We didn't do the floor search there."

"Can I go with you? Somehow, I feel Rapid Creek is the likely location. The Stallings gave a description of the man feeding them and it could have been Boyd Silver."

"Why don't we meet you there?"

Ox buzzed Angel. "I know I just got in, but now I've got to scoot back out. Anything on the schedule that can't be changed?"

"I'll manage it."

When Ox walked into Rapid Creek, the guard asked, "Are you Reverend Christie?"

"Yes."

"They're in the basement."

In the basement, he saw Silver unlocking the last door down the hallway. He looked into the first room just as the police were coming out.

"Would you mind if I asked Silver a few questions?" he asked Oster.

"By all means. I'll accompany you."

Silver looked alarmed when they passed the other rooms and approached him. "Mr. Silver," said Ox, "do you remember Mr. and Mrs. Stallings?"

"I'm afraid not."

"They remember you."

"From where?"

"From seeing you looking down on them."

"Nonsense."

"And they weren't always completely unconscious when they were on the second floor and got shots. They saw the aide and they saw you. Now we know there's an underground room in this basement. You probably put them there when we began searching the units upstairs. When we find it in a few minutes, you will be in serious trouble."

"Search all you want to. I've got work to do. I'll be in my office."

Oster grabbed Silver's arm. "You'll be here." He pushed him into the next room.

Ox watched Silver. The man was so nervous, he was trembling. He kept shifting his eyes. He looked like he would start running any minute. "I need to go to the bathroom," he said.

"Do it in your pants," said Oster.

They moved into the paint room, Oster pushing Silver ahead of him.

"I need to sit down," said Silver. He flopped down on the pile of drop cloths in the corner. "I feel dizzy."

Ox said to Oster, "We'll definitely want to see what's under those drop cloths."

"Right."

Emmett played his flashlight inch by inch on the floor. He tugged on the shelf units to see if any would swing out like the one in Daniels' safe. Oster walked slowly toward the pile of drop cloths. Silver closed his eyes as if dozing off. Oster stopped in front of Silver and leaned forward.

"I'll give you one last chance, Silver. Where is Starky-Stallings?"

"How would I know?"

To Emmett, "Yank his sorry hide out of the way."

Emmett and Oster both grabbed Silver and heaved him up. Silver stumbled across the room toward the door, but Jessie May blocked him in.

Ox, Oster, and Emmett removed the pile of drop cloths, revealing a trap door. Emmett opened it and shined his light down.

"She's here."

CHAPTER SIXTY-FOUR

Oster charged across the room. "Jessie May, call for an ambulance." He grabbed Silver and slammed him against a shelf unit. "Put your hands behind you, now." He cuffed him and slammed him to the floor. "Don't move from there."

Ox and Emmett were already in the hidden room. "I don't feel any pulse," said Ox.

Emmett placed his cheek against Cecelia's mouth. "Might be some breath. Can't be sure."

"We've got to get her out of here."

"I'll get up above. If you can lift her up to me, I'll pull her up," said Emmett. He climbed out.

Ox lifted her up, and Emmett reached down, grabbed her, and very gently, pulled her up. "Put her on some of those drop cloths," said Oster. He leaned over, felt her wrist and placed his other hand near her mouth. "Can't be sure if she's alive. The paramedics will know."

In the ambulance, two paramedics worked on her. At the hospital, the ER doctor said, "She's alive, but just barely."

Soon, dextrose was dripping into her. An oxygen mask

covered her mouth and nose. Silver said, "I have to call The Group so they can get someone out here to run the place."

"Do it, and do it quick."

Silver called. "I'm under arrest. You need to get someone here to cover for me. They found Susan Starky and they blame me."

Oster grabbed the phone and slammed it into the cradle. "You had the key, jackass." He cuffed him again and shoved him through the door. "You're going to have a nice vacation."

Willis Taylor watched Silver maintain his balance down the front steps. He walked into Ann Cooke's unit and told her about it. "If anybody's second in command here, it's you," he said.

"Let's just do our jobs and try to keep things running for the sake of the patients," she said. "There will be a substitute here soon enough."

Hayley Buchanan paid a visit to Health Crest Nursing Home. Even though it was out of her jurisdiction, she wanted to see for herself. She spotted a nurse inside the front entrance.

"I'm looking for Miss Upchurch."

"That's me. Who are you?"

"I'm Hayley Buchanan, Assistant District Attorney. I have a packet of last wills and testaments from here. They were turned over to me with the statement that you coerced your patients to sign them."

Miss Upchurch's face turned crimson. She shouted, "Who stole those from us? No one was forced to sign." She looked like she was ready to attack.

"A witness watched you force a patient to sign, keeping him up late into the night until he was so tired he was ready to drop. You'll have your chance to refute the charges in court."

"Which one of our patients made that false claim?" shouted Miss Upchurch.

"It wasn't a patient." Hayley Buchanan turned and left. Now she would turn the papers over to the local authorities.

CHAPTER SIXTY-FIVE

At police headquarters, interrogations were going on in three rooms. Daniels was in one, Silver was in another, and Rosenfeld was in the third. Each knew the others were being questioned by the same team. Each was apprehensive about what the others were saying. Each was being offered a certain amount of immunity if they cooperated. They knew Starky had been found alive. It was only a matter of time before she would talk. Oster invited Ox to watch the charade from the observation room. "Let me know if you have any suggestions for questions to these bozos."

At first, the three were unanimous in stating they didn't know what the interrogator was talking about. Starky was a complete mystery to them.

The crack began to appear when the interrogator said to Silver, "What if I told you Daniels blamed you for Starky's abduction and said you buried her in that room in the paint shop?"

"I didn't know anything about that. That was all Daniels."

"But you had the key to the paint shop."

"Daniels had keys to everything."

"How did he get her in without you knowing?"

"He must have come in through the side door or maybe at night."

"Didn't that door have an alarm on it, and weren't there always guards?"

"Maybe through the front door."

"Wasn't there a guard there?"

"Maybe the guard took a break."

"That Daniels must be pretty clever to get Starky in there without you knowing."

"I just do as I'm told."

"How often did you see Mr. Bush?"

"I never saw him."

"He didn't come to Rapid Creek?"

"Why would he?"

"Rosenfeld said you selected patients for him to operate on."

"Bush made those selections."

"How could Bush make the selections if he didn't come in . . . if he didn't know the patients? How did he know they needed surgery?"

"I don't know. He kept all the records."

"Who gave him the daily patient progress records?"

"I don't know how he decided who to send to surgery and who not to. I just did as I was told."

"If you did something illegal because you were told to, you are guilty of doing something illegal. Do you want to help us stop something illegal and get credit for it? Or do you want to go down with a sinking ship?"

"I didn't do anything wrong. Daniels, Bush and Rosenfeld made the decisions. I was just the supplier."

"What were you supplying?"

"I don't know, just sick patients."

"You supplied sick patients. Did any of them ever get well?"

"Bush has the records."

"That's not what Daniels says. And Rosenfeld backs him up."

"They are both liars. I just followed orders."

"I'll get back to you. Too bad. I gave you a chance."

The team then moved to Rosenfeld. The interrogator asked, "What happened to the organs you removed from patients?"

"Diseased organs were disposed of in the incinerator."

"What happened to the good organs you removed?"

"Am I under arrest?"

"Not yet."

"I want my lawyer. I'm not answering anymore questions without him here."

"Too bad. Looks like you'll be the one taking the rap."

"What do you mean?"

"You mean to say you really don't know what they were doing with those organs?"

"I don't know."

"Daniels and Silver say you knew. Daniels says he had no idea what you and Bush were up to."

"That Daniels is a liar. He gave the order for organs."

"Who selected the donor?"

"I'm not answering anymore questions."

"Your funeral."

The team left the room and went into the observation area. They sat and watched the three men.

Oster leaned over to Ox. "They'll let them sweat for a while. They'll leave Daniels alone while they work on the other two. Daniels has the most to lose. He'll get the book thrown at him, but the other two won't be far behind."

"Silver knows the Stallings couple was kept on the second floor. They remember him between shots when the haze was lifting."

Oster walked over to the team and relayed that. In a few moments, the team was back with Silver.

"Starky's parents remember you. They will testify that you held them prisoner on your second floor, drugging them constantly so Starky would do as she was told. It proves you were in complete collusion with Daniels, Rosenfeld, and Bush. Do you think Bush is going to accept the blame when we catch him? Are you really going to play along with them and go down with them? I thought you were an administrator. I thought you had some sense."

"I was told to keep them there. I didn't know why. I just did what I was told to do."

"Who told you?"

"Bush. It was Bush. He told me."

"That's not what Daniels says."

"I don't care what that liar says. Okay, I knew Starky was down there. Daniels brought her in. That's when I learned about the room in the paint shop. And I knew about Mr. and Mrs. Stallings. I just did as I was told."

"We'll get all that typed up and you can sign it. We'll proceed to bring charges against Daniels for abduction and attempted murder. We appreciate your help."

Silver looked completely confused. The team left.

CHAPTER SIXTY-SIX

At Temple University Hospital, an intensive care nurse checked the dextrose drip leading into Cecelia Stallings' arm. She adjusted the oxygen mask. The electrocardiogram showed an extremely weak heart pattern. A cardiology resident studied it and shook his head.

"Damn near comatose."

"She hasn't shown any change," said the nurse. "She might or might not make it."

There had been heavy rain for two days. A black BMW was pulled out of the Schuylkill River near Passyunk Avenue. The window on the driver's side was rolled down. There was no one in the car. It was registered to Joseph Bush. His outdated driver's license was in the glove compartment. It was difficult to tell where the car had entered the water. It could have been pushed by the swollen current from farther north.

The Nursing Home Watch Committee meeting ended. Oster, Emmett, and Jessie May stayed afterward to run over some ideas with Ox.

Ox had been thinking about The Group. The only two functioning members of the board were Brame and Suggs. Pressing those two could really put a squeeze on the operation. They were as guilty as Daniels, Slawson, and Bush when it came to patient abuse.

"I'm sure I can get warrants to search their houses," said Oster.

"It might be a good idea to search them simultaneously. I keep thinking Slawson has to be somewhere," said Ox.

"If you want to join us in that," said Oster, "you can go with me to one, and Emmett and Jessie May can take the other."

"Count me in," said Ox. "Just let me know when so I can juggle church meetings and some counseling appointments."

"We'll have to start calling you Officer Reverend," said Oster. "By the way, we learned Slawson was originally from Richmond, Virginia. Actually, he was from Henrico County, just outside of Richmond. The police down there are on the lookout for him. We'll get him eventually."

"Do you think Bush drowned?"

"Hard to say. Since the window was neatly rolled down, he could have staged it. We'll keep looking. If he uses his credit cards, we'll be on it. Same with his bank account. Eventually, something more than his car will surface."

"The overall operation is pretty well shut down with Daniels and Rosenfeld being held. I have the feeling that Silver, while guilty, was a follower rather than a leader," said Ox.

"Yep," said Oster.

"What about some of the other nursing home administrators?"

"It's apparent that they are simply doing their jobs. They are actually being administrators. Silver was just cooling his heels in his office and letting Bush push the buttons. I think they hired him because he was too dumb to question anything. That Mockler was actually doing a decent job in spite of Bush's monkey business. I think the others were, too," said Oster.

"I get the impression Bush was transferring patients from

the four homes to Rapid Creek when it became apparent they had no one to check on them. From Rapid Creek they were forwarded to Night and Day and Rosenfeld's scalpel, and then back to Rapid Creek for future use. That second floor was the organ resource unit."

"That's what we figure, Reverend," said Oster. "I think I'm going to give you a badge."

"I have a hunch your bosses might not approve."

Jessie May and Emmett had not joined the conversation. They appeared fascinated by the relationship that had developed between Oster and Ox.

"Sarge," said Jessie May, "you had said something about getting some of those nursing home people together to learn more about what was going on. I'd like to suggest Ann Cooke at Rapid Creek. She's not the administrator, but she's got her head screwed on right."

"As a matter of fact, I was thinking of setting up a meeting with her, Willis Taylor, Mockler, and Humphrey. They can be our eyes as to what is going on. And I might add more names from the other nursing homes as I get to know them."

"How are you going to get them together without tipping your hand?" asked Ox.

"I can pull them into headquarters for questioning. That way, the brass can't come down on them."

"Especially if we put pressure on the remaining brass," said Ox. "Is Daniels still denying everything?"

"That jackass is just so innocent to the whole world, the only things he has ever done are eat, sleep, and breathe."

CHAPTER SIXTY-SEVEN

Ox visited Joseph and Marie Stallings. "Cecelia is here in the hospital."

"You found her?" asked Joseph.

"Yes, and you gave me the lead."

"How?"

"You mentioned the trap door room. We modified our search and found her. She's recovering in the intensive care unit."

"Thank God," said Marie.

"Actually, she was in the same room they held you in for a short while. It was at Rapid Creek Nursing Home. The man you described was Boyd Silver, the administrator. He is now in custody."

"That was quick," said Joseph.

"Thank you," said Marie. "Thank you."

When Oster called Ann Cooke, she asked, "Can we meet here? I don't want to be away from my patients too long. We could meet in Silver's office. There's still no substitute for him here."

"I think that can be arranged. I can have the others picked up."

Mockler had no problem being gone a few hours. He

had everything under control even if he was short-staffed. Humphrey had no problem either. He had little to do even before the reduced activity at Night and Day. Police cruisers picked them up and brought them to Rapid Creek.

"You may think this is an unusual group," said Oster, "a guard, an aide, an administrator, and a receptionist, but you represent three of the six nursing homes owned by The Group. I know that all four of you are concerned about the things that have been going on. I would like to give you each my card and ask that you call the minute anything odd or unusual or questionable takes place in your nursing home. We are looking for Mr. Slawson. He is vice-president of The Group. Mr. Daniels is currently being held. Mr. Bush has disappeared. Dr. Rosenfeld is being held for questioning. A lot is going on."

"What do you want of us?" asked Mockler.

"I want you to be my eyes at your place. It's that simple. We can't be everywhere."

"Sergeant," said Ann Cooke, "I get the feeling that most of the operation has come to a stop."

"That's true, but two of The Group could get things moving again, and Bush could show up. We want him. We're thinking of posting police at all six of the nursing homes and at the homes of The Group board members."

"Willis and I will be watching everything at Rapid Creek. Can we call at any time, day or night?" asked Ann Cooke.

"Twenty-four seven," said Oster.

The interrogation of Merton Daniels continued. "Mr. Silver has given us a written statement that you abducted Cecelia Stallings, imprisoned her, and left her to die. Do you wish to change your statement?"

"I am not guilty."

"Miss Stallings is now recovering in the intensive care unit. She will be capable of making a clear statement regarding the abduction and imprisonment."

"I did not abduct her and did not imprison her."

"Well, it doesn't make much difference what you say, given the witnesses. And even if you didn't abduct her, you will be facing enough charges to provide you with several life terms in prison."

"I'm not guilty of any wrongdoing, and you can't prove otherwise. I want my attorney, and I want out of here. No more questions."

CHAPTER SIXTY-EIGHT

Oster decided to visit another of the six nursing homes. He picked Healthy Acres. He asked Ox if he wanted to go with him. The record showed the administrator to be Louis Giardinelli.

Giardinelli was downright unfriendly. "What goes on here is not the business of the Philadelphia Police."

Oster was more unfriendly. "What goes on here is my business, you donkey. And if I hear you braying anymore, I'll search your house, your mother's house, and your girlfriend's house. Get off your butt and give me a tour. And, oh yes, I have a search warrant."

Giardinelli gave him a tour, but he wasn't verbose. "This is the first floor."

They walked through three wings. One wing was for patients, two in a room. They were reasonably alert and seemed to be properly cared for. Ox checked and found the water pitchers were full. They were actually cold. Bed linens seemed clean. The bathrooms had clean towels, soap, and toilet paper.

A pattern developed. Giardinelli stood in the hall, impatiently. Ox stood in the doorway, looking. Oster checked everything in each room.

Another wing included the kitchen and a small dining room for the staff. The kitchen was clean.

"Not bad," said Ox.

Several nurse aides watched. The men moved on. "This is the second floor."

The patient rooms were the same in all respects, with one exception. All of the patients were asleep.

Ox asked Giardinelli, "Why the big difference between the first-floor patients and the second-floor patients?"

"What difference?"

"On the first floor the patients were alert. On the second floor they were all asleep. Why is that?"

"We put patients who get visitors on the first floor. It makes it more convenient for the visitors."

"There weren't any visitors downstairs, and anyhow, that doesn't explain why the patients who get visitors are more alert."

"I never thought about it. I guess that's just the way it is."

Ox and Oster exchanged glances. Ox said, "Could it be another Rapid Creek second floor?"

There was another difference. On the first floor, there were two aides. On the second, there was only one.

Oster approached the aide. "Do these patients get transferred for surgery?" The aide looked startled. "Some."

Giardinelli was only a few feet away. "Some need surgery. Some have had it. One reason they aren't as alert is that they are recovering."

"Did they have organs removed?" asked Ox.

"If they had diseased organs."

"What if the organs weren't diseased?" asked Ox.

"Why would we need to remove good organs?"

"Maybe they were organ donors," said Oster.

"I wouldn't know."

"You're the administrator, aren't you?" asked Oster.

"I don't decide who needs surgery and who doesn't."

"Who does?" asked Ox.

"Mr. Bush."

Oster turned back to the aide. "How often do you give these patients morphine shots?"

"As needed."

"Many surgical transfers?"

"Not lately."

Ox asked Giardinelli, "Has Bush been in today?"

"Not that I know of."

"Doesn't he check in with you?"

"As far as I know."

"Okay, jerk," said Oster, "I'm going to make sure you join Bush and his friends in a long-term, limited-service hotel. Let's see the rest of your haven for patients."

They went up the steps. "This is the third floor."

CHAPTER SIXTY-NINE

Joe Bush drove an old pickup truck. The left front fender was crumpled, but hung on. The rattletrap overheated if he drove over forty miles an hour. He pulled into a greasy-spoon diner for lunch. It had been a long time since he had eaten food that was an insult to the stomach, but he would just have to get used to it . . . at least for a while.

At Temple University Hospital, an intensive care nurse checked Cecelia Stallings' vital signs again. She shook her head and adjusted the oxygen mask.

"There may be a slight improvement," said the cardiology resident. "It's hard to tell if she'll make it."

Charles Z. Slawson sat in a hot and stuffy room in an old boarding house in the Oakland Section of Pittsburgh. The landlord thought Slawson was a lecturer at the University of Pittsburgh. That would be a step up for the rundown place. There was a wardrobe blocking a door connecting to the next room. It didn't block the transom over the door and loud fiddle music with a heavy drumbeat vibrated through. The adjoining room was occupied by an Irish couple who argued continually.

Across the hall was a strange couple with a dog named Otto. Slawson felt depressed.

Thomas Brame and Donald Suggs were in Joe Bush's office. "I can't figure out his system," said Brame.

"Well, we can't do anything anyhow with the police all over the place," said Suggs. "I thought Bush was going to take care of Christie."

"Who knows where Bush is now."

"Well, I sure don't know how to arrange a Christie accident," said Brame, "and anyhow, like Daniels said, that wouldn't get rid of the police."

"I'm beginning to think we should operate the hospitals legitimately, in accordance to JCAH standards."

"The profit would drop to zip," said Brame.

"We could plan to get back to normal someday, when the heat's off," said Suggs.

"The heat will never be off with Christie around."

Daniels glared at Charles Cheek, his attorney. "Get me out of here."

"Merton," said Cheek, "we've got a load of problems—witnesses, hospital transplant records, and worst of all, Starky. If that Starky girl testifies, you are dead in the water. Just keep denying everything. I'll try to get to the girl. Maybe we can buy her."

"There's still Silver."

"I think we can implicate him. He's not too bright."

"What about that witness in the hospital? She saw me."

"We can make mincemeat out of eye witnesses."

CHAPTER SEVENTY

Cecelia Stallings became aware of something covering her mouth. She didn't know where she was. She was in a bed. There were lights in the ceiling. She wasn't in that dark room with no door. There were nurses. There was a needle in her arm. She was in a hospital. What happened?

A nurse was checking her pulse. "Where am I?"

"Temple University Hospital. How do you feel?"

"How did I get here?"

"You came in by ambulance. Let me call the resident. Be right back."

There were patients on both sides of her. One of them had her eyes open. The other looked asleep. A policeman was standing at the foot of her bed. Then a man was leaning over her.

"I'm Dr. Horowitz. How are you feeling?"

"Okay, I guess."

"You gave us quite a scare."

"How long have I been here?"

"A few weeks. Looks like you'll be going home soon."

Home. Where was home? It came back to her. Night and Day Nursing Home. Her parents. Where were they? Cecelia

254

was panic stricken. She had implicated The Group, and now her parents might be killed. "Please find my parents."

"Miss Stallings, your parents have been found and are safe here in the hospital," said Dr. Horowitz.

"Oh, my Lord, I have a lot to tell the police. Please get them. When can I see my parents?"

"Soon. When we think you are up to it, we will wheel you to their room. They are fine and are thankful you are all right. I'll let the police know you want to talk to them."

ER Nurse Pat Christopher met with Carla Hillman, the administrator of Peoples' Universal Hospital in Harrisburg.

"Miss Hillman, a number of people in the ER were upset by the inundation of patients from the Philadelphia nursing homes. It was more than we could handle. It was a terrible imposition, and what's worse, we couldn't really properly care for those patients."

"I agree."

"You do? Then why? I understand you approved everything."

"I had no choice."

"What do you mean? You're the administrator. You could have closed the ER, diverted the overload to other hospitals."

"I was upset about it, too. I certainly understand why you and others were upset. Some of those patients should have been diverted to other hospitals in Harrisburg and Philadelphia."

"Then why?"

"I guess I can say it now. Mr. Daniels, Chairman of The Group, owners of the hospital, ordered it. Mr. Daniels is now being held by the Philadelphia police. There are a lot of unanswered questions. The Group also owned the nursing homes the patients came from. I better not say anymore."

When Pat Christopher left Carla Hillman's office, she had a new set of worries. What was the future of Peoples' Universal Hospital?

Dr. Rosenfeld was charged with practicing medicine without a license and was held, pending an investigation of the surgeries. The problem was that all the records had been destroyed. The police and the Joint Commission were cooperating in the review of surgical records at Peoples' Universal Hospitals in Harrisburg and Philadelphia.

Slawson's car was spotted, parked on Oakland Avenue, a few blocks from the University of Pittsburgh. There were police staked out, waiting for him to appear.

CHAPTER SEVENTY-ONE

At Ann Cooke's suggestion, patients from the second floor of Rapid Creek Nursing Home were transferred—some to Temple University Hospital, some to Thomas Jefferson University Hospital, and some to Albert Einstein Medical Center—for examination. Doctors discovered that they all had kidneys removed.

Rosenfeld was asked why only kidneys. He said that was his specialty and he was only following orders. When asked whose orders, he said Daniels. He had no idea what happened to the kidneys, other than they were carefully saved and prepared for shipment. He didn't know where they were taken. He said they would have to ask Susan Starky. Bail was set at one million dollars. Rosenfeld wasn't going anywhere.

Cecelia Stallings was interviewed by the police in the hospital. She couldn't testify as to who abducted her. She was unconscious until she woke up in the room without a door. She wasn't told anything about the patients transferred from Rapid Creek to the Night and Day operating room other than they needed surgery, but she had her suspicions.

Emmett remembered Kitty Laker and asked about her. That opened a different door. She was well aware of what happened to Miss Laker. She knew her kidney had been removed and that it was not diseased. It was sent to Peoples' Universal Hospital in Harrisburg. She also knew Miss Laker had died as a result of infection stemming from the surgery. Now Rosenfeld was charged with murder, and Daniels was facing more problems.

Charles Slawson was nervous and decided he would move on. He couldn't stand the fiddle music any longer. Rent was due, so he opened the door and trotted. The police didn't see him until he was in the car. He was almost to Forbes Avenue before they caught up with him. He turned left and in a few minutes turned left again on Dawson.

The police called ahead and he was blocked at the Boulevard. Slawson almost seemed relieved to be caught.

CHAPTER SEVENTY-TWO

Bush's secretary called Oster. "Mr. Brame and Mr. Suggs are in Mr. Bush's office."

"We're on our way," said Oster.

"Why did she let you know?" asked Ox.

"She wants to be sure she's not arrested."

When Ox and Oster arrived, Brame and Suggs were packing records into a box. "Packing those away for safe keeping?" asked Ox.

"Gentlemen," said Oster, "would you please come with us to the police station? We have some questions for you."

Thomas Brame sat the box on the desk. "Unless we are under arrest, we need to get back to work."

"Well, actually," said Oster, "the fact that you are in the process of removing evidence gives me the right to take you in for questioning."

"What evidence?" asked Suggs.

"Don't get smart," said Oster.

"It's not smart."

Ox smiled. It seemed Oster was developing a sense of humor.

"You gentlemen certainly are aware of the problems that have surfaced regarding your nursing home operations and certain transactions with your hospitals Mr. Bush is said to have arranged. It's likely the records of those transactions happen to be in that box you just put on the desk. Thanks for packing them up for us," said Oster. "Now pick it up and follow me to my chariot. Do I have to cuff you?"

In the back seat of the squad car, Suggs and Brame were quiet, each looking out the window on their side.

Ox sat at an angle in the passenger seat so he could see them. He decided to let them feel a little more uneasy. "You two may not know it, but Charles Slawson was caught yesterday in Pittsburgh. I understand he is fully cooperating with the police. Miss Starky, whose real name is Stallings, is cooperating with the police. It looks like the door is closing on your illegal operation."

Neither Suggs nor Brame responded. They both continued to look out the windows. "All those patients with their kidneys removed make it look like you had an illegal transplant business going. Must have been lucrative." Both men looked angry, but said nothing.

"Rosenfeld is being charged with murder. It's hard to imagine that you two were unaware of what was going on. Daniels will be found guilty of murder. So will Slawson. So will Bush, if he's alive. So will you."

Suggs was the first to respond. "We didn't know what Rosenfeld was doing. He took orders from Daniels and Bush."

Oster gave Ox a thumbs up.

"Is that what both of you are claiming?" asked Ox.

"That's exactly right," said Brame.

"Like rats leaving a sinking ship," mumbled Ox.

At that moment, Slawson was being interrogated at police headquarters.

"I didn't know what was going on. Bush and Daniels made all

the decisions. I just followed orders. We give good patient care at our nursing homes and hospitals."

Hilda D'Ablo reported, "The police don't know what to do, so they're arresting everybody they can get their hands on. Typical police brutality."

Her sister added, "It makes it look like they know what they are doing."

CHAPTER SEVENTY-THREE

The door was closing quickly on The Group. Everyone was blaming Daniels and the missing Bush. Oster invited Ox to observe the interrogation of Daniels and all future interrogations having to do with the nursing homes. He sat on the other side of the one-way window.

"Mr. Daniels," said Oster, "Slawson, Suggs, and Brame all blame you for everything. It's hard to imagine how you did it without any of them being involved, but maybe you qualify as a master criminal."

"They are all liars."

"Are you saying they were involved, too?"

"They were. All of them."

"You just agreed they were involved, too. That 'too' is an 'also.' It states you were involved, too."

"I wasn't involved."

"With all the testimony against you from all of them, there's no jury in the world that would find you innocent. Make it easy on yourself and 'fess up. You are just prolonging the agony. You know you will be found guilty."

"If I'm found guilty, the agony will just be beginning."

"Mr. Daniels," said Oster, "if you cooperate with us, we will recommend to the DA that you be spared the death penalty. That's what the others are likely to get."

For a few moments, Daniels said nothing. He looked like he was thinking about it. "I'll discuss it with my attorney."

Ox and Oster had lunch together.

"I have to confess," said Ox, "at one time I thought you were so wrapped up in your own ego that you could hardly see the light of day. I was wrong. You can see the light of day."

Oster laughed. "Well, you weren't so far off the track. I know I've had an ego problem, but sometimes it has to emerge to get others to move faster."

"I can see that."

"Also, I think we all grow with experience. I've done some dumb things in my lifetime. I don't feel as much need for that ego anymore, but thanks for being frank."

"Any time. Thanks for keeping me involved. I knew something was wrong the first time I walked into that Night and Day Nursing Home. As a minister, I felt a need to pursue it. Actually, as a human being, I felt the need to pursue it."

"Maybe ministers are the police of the soul."

"Good way of putting it. Ministers have to keep ego under control too."

CHAPTER SEVENTY-FOUR

Carla Hillman, administrator of Peoples' Universal Hospital in Harrisburg called the police. One of their ambulances was missing. Emmett mentioned it to Ox, who's first thought was Bush.

"Could be," said Emmett.

"If so, does that mean he's heading west?"

"Well, Harrisburg is west and they have a hospital further west in Pittsburgh."

"He'd probably know better than to appear there. They know he's wanted."

"On the other hand," said Emmett, "it could be some kids on a joy ride."

Hours later, the ambulance was found abandoned in Frederick, Maryland. Emmett called Ox.

"Looks like he's heading south, if Bush is the thief."

"Doesn't sound like kids joy riding."

The doctors allowed Cecelia Stallings to be wheeled to the third-floor patient unit conference room at Temple University Hospital. Ox, Oster, Emmett, and Jessie May were waiting for her.

"We know you've been through your own private hell," said Ox, "but things have taken a turn and we need your help."

"I'm finally free to talk," said Cecelia. "My parents are free and so am I."

"What was going on in that green building at Night and Day?" asked Oster.

"Thank God. Now I can talk about it. Bush was holding my parents. If I didn't do as he said, he would kill them. He said he might torture them just for fun. He was running the whole thing for The Group."

"What exactly was going on?" asked Oster.

It took a few moments for her to answer. It was obvious she was tired. "They were removing organs, mainly kidneys, selling them to patients in their hospitals, and also on the black market. It was a lucrative business, taking from the helpless and selling to the desperate. They've piled up millions. Every one of them is a multimillionaire."

"How long was this going on?"

"I was there for over four years. I don't know how long before that. I just thank God I'm free of the place." She had to pause for a few moments. "There were times I wished they would just take my organs and do away with me. It was horrible. I could hear the ambulances come in at all times of the day and night. Each time, I knew some poor soul was being cut open for a kidney and there was no one to help. And eventually they were all killed and cremated. No one cared. Night and day, on and on, kidneys were ripped out of those helpless beings."

"You look tired," said Ox. "We better let you rest."

Cecelia looked relieved. "Thank God my parents are all right. I could envision them being operated on and then burned. Oh, wait, there's something else."

Dr. Horowitz interrupted. "That's enough for now. We need to let her rest or she will have a relapse."

Cecelia closed her eyes as she was wheeled out of the room. Ox, Oster, Emmett, and Jessie May watched her go.

"I wonder what else," said Ox. "What could be any worse than ripping out their organs?"

"Come back in a couple of hours," said Dr. Horowitz. "A stroke now could be fatal."

"I'm for hitting a hamburger joint," said Emmett.

"We ate lunch, but I think Emmett has a tapeworm," said Jessie May.

"Well, that's better than a hoagie joint," said Oster. "They might serve us Emmett's brains."

"I could use a cup of coffee," said Ox. "I'm sure they have a cafeteria here."

"We could visit Mr. and Mrs. Stallings," said Jessie May. "On second thought, no need to bother them."

"Cafeteria it is," said Oster.

In the cafeteria, the constant noise of dishes and chatter made it necessary to talk loud. "They ought to name this the clatterteria," said Emmett.

"That Stallings family has been through hell and back," said Jessie May.

A nurse came over to their table. "Excuse me," she said. "I'm Elizabeth Beasley, the head nurse on the third floor. I saw you with Miss Stallings. When I came on duty this morning, the night nurse told me Miss Stallings keeps having nightmares. She would cry and say, 'I'm doing the best I can. Please don't hurt them.' And her blood pressure would jump from too low to too high. We've been concerned she could have a major stroke. I thought you might want to know. I don't know what she's been through, but I don't think she's out of the woods yet."

"I hope our questioning her isn't going to cause a relapse," said Jessie May. "I have the feeling it will help her if she gets it out in the open," said Ox.

"Well, keep in mind that you need to be gentle with her," said Miss Beasley.

"Thank you," said Oster. "Would you like to join us for lunch?"

"No, thanks, I've got to get back to the floor."

"Well, thanks. Gentle it will be," said Oster. "We'll wait another hour and be back up there."

When they got back to the unit, Dr. Horowitz saw them and went over. "Go on down to the conference room, and we'll see if Miss Stallings is up to it."

They waited another half hour and Miss Beasley stepped in. "We are working on her to get her ready. It may be a few more minutes." Then she stepped out and closed the door behind her.

"Working on her?" said Oster. "I hope she's all right."

They waited another fifteen minutes. Ox was about ready to say they should call it a day when Dr. Horowitz wheeled Cecelia Stallings in. "Don't take too long."

Cecelia managed a weak smile. "I'll be all right."

Oster was surprisingly gentle. "If you get tired, just say the word and we'll come back another time."

"There's something else I wanted to tell you. Organs were the main thing, but they had a side business going. If you check the graveyard, you'll find that the urns for ashes that are buried there are all empty. They processed the ashes for the carbon in them and made diamonds. They made diamonds from the hair of the patients as well. You may have noticed that most of the patients were bald, especially the ones being processed through repeated surgeries. They took their kidneys and their hair and their ashes."

"Wait a minute," said Ox. "You mean they had a process for converting ashes and hair to diamonds? That sounds unbelievable. How and when did this take place?"

"I guess it's not well known. Under extreme heat and pressure, carbon from hair and ashes can be converted to diamonds. I don't know where the equipment is now, but it was in the back building in the basement. They removed it all when your pressure began to build up."

"Is that where the diamonds came from in all their rings, tie tacks, and cufflinks?" asked Ox.

"Yes. They were a kind of reward for themselves. Actually, you can do an internet search for ashes and diamonds and see the process described."

"We've searched their houses. I think we would have noticed if the equipment was there," said Emmett.

"They might have put it all in storage somewhere," said Ox. "Where did they market the diamonds?" asked Oster.

"I have no idea."

"We should check if there are gift shops in their hospitals," said Jessie May.

"They would have to be careful where they peddled them," said Ox. "It could certainly raise questions."

"This is incredible," said Jessie May. "I never heard of such a thing . . . diamonds from hair and ashes."

"This is so incredible, we might be able to get the press interested. They might even do a feature story," said Ox.

"I'll have our Public Relations Department issue a press release," said Oster. "What about TV?"

"Good idea. I'll push PR."

PR left nothing out. Patient admissions at all of The Group's hospitals stopped dead.

JCAH canceled their accreditation. Law firms experienced a

deluge of clients seeking damages for relatives. The State inspectors descended on the hospitals.

Brame and Suggs were overwhelmed by photographers and reporters. With Bush's disappearance, they had to take care of basic operations in the nursing homes. They managed to complete the payroll, but other bills went unpaid. The electric company threatened to cut off services, but held off, knowing that patients might suffer.

Other nursing homes were suddenly overwhelmed with admission requests from the six under siege by the state and the press. Those patients without families stayed put. Health and Human Services were stymied as to what to do. The state stepped in and took over all six of them.

Elmer and Ox visited Rebecca. Humphrey walked with them. "Are you going to move Miss Rhine out?"

"Not yet, but soon," said Elmer.

"I hope you find a good place."

"It's a new place. It'll be ready in a few weeks."

Rebecca was happier than usual. The aide on the floor was even friendly. She popped in to ask if Rebecca needed anything.

"Things have changed here," said Rebecca. "I'm sorry Kitty isn't here to see it."

"Too bad about her," said Ox. "I wonder if we could have done anything to help."

"Don't blame yourselves," said Rebecca.

"Yes," said Elmer. "Things have to get better in all the nursing homes. There's a long way to go."

"Yes, and now we need to push all the harder. The press has given a lot of credit to the nursing home watch programs. Now when we approach a nursing home, they let us in."

The three major TV stations picked up on it. Each tried to outdo the others with "exclusive" coverage seen "only on their stations." Bush's picture was projected through the morning, afternoon, and evening newscasts.

The six nursing homes became the "victims" for a change. Camera crews showed up unannounced. The state was in the process of completely revamping, increasing staff, and relocating patients to other nursing homes or, in some cases, to hospitals. Day after day, the stories poured out.

TV news hours in other cities picked up on the stories, and nursing homes, in general, became subject to journalists paying visits. Then a call came from Charlotte, North Carolina. Bush had been sighted at a bus station. His picture was rebroadcast in all the adjoining states. State police were on the lookout.

Brame and Suggs were arrested and questioned. Ultimately, they found themselves in court facing murder charges. They both pleaded innocent. They said they had no idea Bush was engineering the organ transplant, and as far as the diamond production, they thought the claim was preposterous. Bail was set at fifty thousand each. It was posted immediately and both men were told not to leave the area.

Immediately, they were both gone.

The D'Ablo sisters reported on the obvious success of the police.

"Well, it just goes to show you. You can put a blind pig out to pasture, and he'll find breakfast."

CHAPTER SEVENTY-FIVE

Joe Bush was on a bus with a ticket to Chicago. He sat on the back seat that ran from side to side in the rear of the bus. He parked himself in the corner and buried his face in a newspaper. A couple of teenagers sat at the other end of the seat. The bus was about half full. Bush was not a happy man. None of his political friends had offered to help. The least they could have done was gotten him a fake ID, but they weren't friends anymore. He was no longer of any value to them.

In his money belt, wallet, and inside coat pocket, he had a hundred and fifty thousand dollars. He would bounce back and then they would be sorry. He still had some old connections in Chicago. He would lay low and let his hair grow long. It would cover his damned pointed ears. A beard would help, too.

He would definitely be back to pay off some personal debts.

At Rapid Creek Nursing Home, Ann Cooke was made Director of Nursing. It had become obvious to state personnel that she was competent and well-motivated. It was made clear to her the state didn't know how long they would keep Rapid Creek open, but she knew it would look good on her resume. The first thing she did was fire Phyllis Davis, the aide on the second floor.

Miss Davis was just leaving when Emmett and Jessie May entered.

"Just the person we were looking for," said Jessie May. "Miss Davis, you are under arrest for assisting in the illegal kidney transplant scam."

Emmett cuffed her. Miss Davis never said a word. They shoved her into the backseat of the squad car and transported her to the police station.

Oster asked her, "Did Silver tell you to give morphine to all those patients?"

"Silver didn't know nothing."

"Then who?"

"Bush. He told me what to do."

"Did you know they were having their kidneys removed?"

"Yes."

"Did you know what would happen to them when both kidneys were removed?"

"When they left the second time, they didn't come back."

"What happened to them?"

"I don't know."

"What would be your guess?"

"I guess they died."

"But you still did what he told you."

"That was my job."

"So you got paid to help kill people."

"I wouldn't say that."

"You just did. You're in big trouble."

"I only did what I was told."

"By the way, did you cut their hair?"

"They were like that when they came back from surgery."

"Did you ask why?"

"I figured it was part of the surgery."

"You'll be held in our nice cell until the judge decides what to do with you."

CHAPTER SEVENTY-SIX

Sergeant Oster dropped by Rapid Creek to see Ann Cooke. The first patient room on the first floor had been converted into her office.

"Miss Cooke, I would like to recommend you for the Police Academy, if you are interested. It's something to think about. This place may be shut down."

"This place is likely to be shut down, and it should be. And my position is not permanent, but it could be a springboard into something at another nursing home."

"That's possible, but your association with this place could have the reverse effect."

"Well, I'll certainly think about it. I appreciate your confidence."

"It would never be boring."

"You got anything for Willis Taylor?"

"I'm working on it."

Next, Oster dropped in at Night and Day to see Humphrey.

"Humphrey, are you content on staying in this no-good job or would you like to attend the Police Academy?"

"I'm an ex-con. You sure they would have me?"

"I'll recommend you. My judgment will count for something."

"Well, it'll be a terrible sacrifice, but I'd do it for the good of mankind." He grinned.

"Yeah," said Oster.

Ox sat in on the Nursing Home Watch Committee meeting.

Elmer reported, "We're getting a lot more cooperation from nursing homes, largely due to the publicity on TV and in the newspapers. Our own home is almost complete. We will be in operation in another week."

Ox could hardly listen. Bush was free. No one knew where he was. What Bush might do kept running through his mind. He imagined what Bush would do to keep from being caught.

When the meeting was over, he asked Oster to stay for a while.

In his office, Ox said, "I've been running over the possibilities of Bush's tactics to avoid being caught. First of all, I don't think he would leave the country. He would lose too much. Not only that, he will want revenge. He can't do that if he skips out of the country. In order for him to stay, he will have to change his appearance. He has too much ego to alter his face. The easiest way for him to change appearance would be to forget the neat haircut. He would let it grow, probably all the way to his shoulders. And he would grow a beard. He might wear glasses, plain ones."

"You're probably right."

"Why not have an artist enhance his picture with hair and beard, and distribute to police stations all over the country."

"Easily done."

"But it shouldn't be released to the public. He would change tactics."

"Sounds like a plan, Detective Christie."

"I had another thought."

"I'm not surprised."

"What's his background? Where was he from originally? Would he head back there? Would he have friends from years past?"

"We can check that out."

"Another thing. He was last seen in that bus station in Charlotte, North Carolina. What buses left that station that day? The odds are he was on one of them."

"Makes sense. I think you missed your calling."

"I have a vested interest. I suspect Mr. Bush will want to bushwhack me and my family."

CHAPTER SEVENTY-SEVEN

Joe Bush sat by the window, looking out at the lake. He was in a small motel on Lake Shore Drive in Chicago. He had made three phone calls. None of them were working numbers any longer. He was on his own.

He decided he might as well head east. No one knew where he was. Philadelphia would be the last place anyone would think to look for him. He had to do something about his appearance, especially the ears. The pointed tops had to go, even if that meant surgery. Whatever happened would be an improvement.

Bush thumbed through the phone book. He called and made an appointment with a plastic surgeon. The man guaranteed him he could make his ears round. He was scheduled for the following Monday. He stared out the window until it got dark. He ordered room service even though it was unlikely anyone was looking for him in Chicago. At eleven o'clock, he watched the news. He switched from one station to another just to be sure there was nothing about him.

Oster left the Temple University Hospital Security Office and drove over to Rapid Creek.

He found Willis Taylor coming down the steps from the second floor.

"You have an interview scheduled at Temple Hospital for a job on the security staff."

The interview at Temple took all of five minutes. Willis filled out a form and was given two uniforms and was told to report to the Emergency Room Guard Station the following morning at seven—at almost double the salary he was paid at Rapid Creek.

Jessie May put the phone down. "There were fourteen buses scheduled out of Charlotte the day Bush was there."

"Great," said Emmett. "He was probably on one of them."

"One was to Philadelphia. We can probably forget that one. Here's the list."

"Well, there are TV stations in all of them. They'll probably all show the undoctored picture of Bush," said Emmett.

"The whole batch, doctored and not, will be transmitted to the police stations."

"Those buses were headed east, west, north, and south. He could be almost anywhere."

"Except here," said Jessie May.

CHAPTER SEVENTY-EIGHT

Ox stood behind the pulpit and looked out at his congregation. The church was full, as usual, but there was an undercurrent of excitement. He knew it was from the TV and newspaper accounts of the nursing home scandals and the church's involvement. He could recall when there was only a sprinkling of members each Sunday. Now, the church was full of people who were active doers, people who gave and helped. He began his sermon.

"Never underestimate the power of people doing what is right to stamp out evil. This is power to overcome any obstacle. Some of you have been involved in the Nursing Home Watch Program. More are joining in.

"You've seen the TV stories and have read the newspaper accounts about the nursing home abuse in this area. This church was instrumental in exposing and stopping this monstrous activity, torturing people for profit.

"The Germantown Unitarian Church also has a nursing home watch program. Ours is patterned after theirs and now other churches are joining in. Because of the public attention, nursing homes are more cooperative. There are some nursing homes that provide good care.

"There are a number that don't. In some cases, it's because the owners are greedy. In others, it's brought about by poor selection of employees. We've discovered that some nursing homes neglect to run proper background checks during the hiring process. This has allowed a few sadistic individuals to come in contact with helpless people with some horrible consequences. Hopefully, this practice is now undergoing correction.

"Nursing home watch programs save lives and prevent horrible abuse. Residents can recuperate or live out their lives in peace. Our own home opens officially this afternoon. Elmer's niece will be the first occupant. It will be open to any member of our church who needs it. This applies to members of our sister churches as well.

"Our church newsletter will give you periodic reports on the progress. I want to stress that members of this church have made life better for literally thousands of people in this area."

Ox had members of the Nursing Home Watch Program stand up and invited more to join at the meeting after the service.

The following day in Chicago, Joe Bush had outpatient surgery on his ears, removing the points so they would be round like normal ears as soon as the swelling went down. He left the hospital with both ears bandaged. The day after, his picture was televised in all the cities on the bus routes out of Charlotte, including Chicago. The surgeon saw the picture and called the police, reporting the surgery. This news was televised all over the country. Bush was now national news. He would have liked to kill the surgeon.

Nonetheless, on another bus, he headed east and found a motel just outside Detroit. He decided to stay in the room, ordering room service so as to be seen by as few people as possible. As Ox had predicted, Bush let his hair grow. It was a slow process as far as any significant change in appearance was concerned. The beard was another matter. It grew much faster and did manage to give him a different appearance with a cursory glance.

The motel was happy to have him. Cash payment was always better than credit cards and he was a heavy tipper. He planned to stay for at least three weeks. By then, his picture would no longer be seen in living rooms across the country.

Lieutenant Governor Ed Stuart called Elliott Johnson, Director of Health and Human Services, and Miss Hahn to his office.

"I've asked you both here because I just read the performance evaluation given to Miss Hahn. It was all excellent. I don't know anyone that excellent, and I know Miss Hahn is anything but excellent."

"I do my job according to the rules and regulations," said Miss Hahn.

"You do just enough to get by. This nursing home fiasco should never have happened. You've allowed thousands of poor souls to be tormented in a living hell. You don't deserve to be in this job. Elliot, get rid of her and change the system. Stop letting the nursing homes know when you will be inspecting."

"I see the wisdom in changing the system," said Johnson, "but I'm not sure I can fire Miss Hahn. She has excellent performance evaluations. I have no grounds."

"Good Lord, man. Haven't you seen the TV reports? Haven't you read the newspapers? Does the governor's office have to tell you how to do your job? This farce of a system has to go."

"I agree with that, but Miss Hahn didn't have the authority to change it."

"She could have stepped forward and said the system doesn't work."

"What if we ask her to design a new system?"

The lieutenant governor sat, looking at Johnson and Hahn. Finally, he said, "All right, Miss Hahn, develop a system that does the job. Have it in my office one week from today."

"One week?" asked Hahn.

"One week. Not a day longer."

CHAPTER SEVENTY-NINE

Ox was busy working on a sermon about personal development and how people grow mentally as they grow older. He thought of the dumb things he had done in childhood, young adulthood, and on to the present. He wondered what he would look back on in ten years and muse on about his current dumbness.

He gazed out of the window and at the traffic on the Schuylkill Parkway far below. A light snow began to fall. He turned on the small TV set in his study and switched to the weather station. They were running storm stories. Maybe if he kept it on long enough, they would give the weather prediction.

He tried to focus on the sermon again. He wondered if he could identify the dumbest thing he had ever done. He had a lot of memories to pull from. Maybe he should think about smart things instead of dumb. Maybe he should think about both for contrast.

It was four o'clock. He switched to the local station for news. They would give a weather report. The big news of the day was the first snowfall. A half inch was predicted. Ox wondered how that could be the big news when there were wars going on.

There was a knock on the door, and Oster peeked in. "Got a minute?"

"What's new?"

"Someone said they saw a man who looked like Bush in Detroit."

"That's closer than Chicago."

"Maybe he's planning a visit. Thought you should know."

"Maybe he likes my sermons."

"We'll be on the lookout to give him some guidance."

"I should make you an honorary minister."

"I thought you would be interested in knowing we picked up Brame and Suggs. The two dumbbells were resting in a restaurant in Manayunk. They must have thought it wasn't part of Philadelphia. Bush is the holdout, but we'll get him."

The state closed down Rapid Creek. The patients who had had kidneys removed were all hospitalized. The others were transferred to a variety of nursing homes, but not to any of the other five. The building became a homeless shelter.

Bishop Markham and Reverend Darner were listening to the news report.

"Well, there's no doubt about it. We will suggest nursing home watch programs for all of our churches," said the bishop.

"Thank goodness for Christie," said Reverend Darner.

CHAPTER EIGHTY

Bush combed his hair to create bangs in front. He cut it himself. It gave him a significantly different look. He walked into the bus station, confident that no one would recognize him. His ears were healed, although still a little red on top. He bought a ticket to Cleveland and sat on a bench off to the side in the waiting room. He didn't have long to wait. Soon, he sat in an almost full bus, next to a window and didn't speak to the man sitting next to him.

In Cleveland, he walked a few blocks and found a hotel. He no longer felt it necessary to avoid other people, but he still kept to himself and stayed in his room. It began to snow, and he watched from his window.

CHAPTER EIGHTY-ONE

Bush took a bus to Pittsburgh. He hated being jostled, especially by big-mouthed teenagers who seemed to be on the way back from some kind of outing. When he stepped off the bus in downtown Pittsburgh, he was in a rotten mood. He hated the city even though he'd never been there before. He bought a ticket for Philadelphia. He waited in the bus station for three hours with what he considered to be the dregs of society. It was all the fault of that Christie and his stupid church. Taking a bus was beneath him. He hadn't had to rely on busses for years. The bus kept making stops in crappy little places to pick up stupid peasants. It was taking too long.

He had to ride with stupid people. He was seething. He got off the bus in Center City, Philadelphia and left the bus station as quickly as possible. It was like he could catch a disease just by being there. What had happened to him? This was his city.

He caught a bus heading north on Broad Street. Then the bus turned east. He got off and walked back to Broad. It was getting dark. He headed west toward the river and the bridge.

Christie would be sorry he was ever born.

He stopped to rest, leaning against a building. A police car slowed down. Bush stood as though he had other business and the car went on slowly past. He backtracked, looking for a cab. He saw one and shouted the address for the church as he jumped into the backseat. They went across the bridge and onto the Schuylkill Expressway, then up, up, up. He couldn't see the river, but he could see the string of lights on the Expressway below.

The driver looked at him in the rearview mirror. "What's the Church of the One Soul? You a minister?"

"Yeah. I'm going to teach them."

"You giving a sermon?"

"A sermon to end all sermons. A sermon of fire."

"Really?" The driver seemed proud to be talking to a minister. "You gonna lay it on them. No more sinning."

"I'm going to scorch men, women, and children." Bush laughed.

The driver looked at Bush. He was beginning to think something was wrong. He wasn't watching where he was going and hit the guardrail. The car was suddenly hanging over the rail with little but steep hillside below. The driver opened his door and got out. The car was about to tumble down the hill to the expressway and the string of traffic below. Bush moved to the left side of the car and reached for the door. His motion tipped the car even more. The car tipped and began to fall. Bush dove out and grabbed a piece of the remaining railing. The car crashed down the hill toward the expressway.

"You stupid fool," shouted Bush.

"There goes my car," shouted the driver. He jumped around frantically.

Bush pulled himself up and began to run up the hill. The driver evidently thought that was the thing to do, so he did, too. Then he turned and ran back down.

Bush was out of breath. He'd bumped his head and it hurt. He stopped to rest, bending over and feeling sick. He sat to get hold of himself. After a while, he heard sirens from the expressway below. "I've got to get that Christie," he muttered.

He stood up and began to walk slowly up the hill.

"The D'Ablo Hour" has been cut to a half hour," said Emmett. "Why does the station even keep them on the air?"

"Advertisers," said Jessie May. "And nut cases like it. Money talks."

"I wish money would shut up."

CHAPTER EIGHTY-TWO

Bush was near the top. He was exhausted. It seemed like every bone in his body was rebelling. He sat by the road. It was a cool night, but he was sweating.

A ramshackle old van heading down the hill stopped. "Hey, buddy. You need a ride?"

Bush pointed up the hill and shook his head.

"That's alright. We'll take you up."

Two men got out and dragged him to the van. They tossed him in on the floor and sat on him.

"Take off," one of them said.

The van headed down the hill. In the back, the two men ripped at Bush's clothing. "Here's the wallet. What else you got?"

"Man, he's loaded. Look what I found in his jacket."

"Man, we won't never have to work again."

"I like them shoes."

"Let me up. What are you doing?"

"Shut up, man, or I'll shut you up."

"Take that jacket. It'll fit somebody."

"We can sell them shoes."

"Hey, look at that ring. Looks like a diamond. Bet that will fit me."

"I'll flip you for it."

"And the cufflinks."

At the bottom of the hill, northbound traffic was at a standstill, but there was no southbound traffic.

"Must be an accident back there somewhere." The van picked up speed.

"He got anything else?"

"Not unless it's in his underwear."

Bush couldn't move because they were sitting on him. "I'll get the police on you."

"Hey, man. We ain't afraid of no police."

"Get rid of him."

"You mean just toss him out?"

"Open the door and get rid of him."

The door opened. Bush grabbed his wallet from the floor. They threw him out. "Be sure to call the police."

Bush hit the pavement head first at fifty miles an hour. He tumbled and rolled for a good fifty feet and slammed up against a street lamp. After that, there was no movement. One leg stuck out onto the roadway.

A fire truck and two ambulances streaked by, north on the southbound lane. After another fifteen minutes, they streaked back. After a while, a police cruiser stopped. Two policemen got out and looked at the bloody mess of a man. One of them called for an ambulance.

Bush woke up. He didn't know where he was. A nurse looked at him.

"Oh, so you decided to wake up."

Bush could hear something whirring in his head. It was music. The world was moving in a circle around him. It moved so fast he couldn't catch up. There was light above or around and it was moving, moving, moving.

"I'm the night nurse. How do you feel?"

Bush closed his eyes to escape the dizzy world.

"Maybe you can understand what I'm saying. You are at the University of Pennsylvania Hospital. Apparently, you were the victim of a hit-and-run. Now that you are awake, I'll call the doctor."

The world kept moving around and around. Soon a doctor came in. He took Bush's pulse. "How are you feeling?"

All Bush heard was tinkling rain.

"You don't have to answer now. You were in an accident. You are at the University of Pennsylvania Hospital. The police found an empty wallet nearby. Is your name Joseph Bush?"

Bush's head throbbed with flashes of light. "Well, that's alright. It'll come back to you."

The doctor looked at the nurse. "Call me if he seems to regain his senses."

For three days, Bush remained in the bed. Finally, the doctor decided there was nothing more he could do for him.

"He's a basket case, but there's nothing else we can do for him here. Move him to a nursing home/rehab unit. He's basically brain-dead. If nothing else, his organs might help someone else, if we can find relatives. Failing that, we might be able to get a judge to approve."

Bush was moved by ambulance to a southwest Philadelphia nursing home that always seemed anxious for new patients.

A nurse and a nurse aide looked down at him.

"We sure get some winners in here," said the aide. "His mouth looks all dried out with them cracked lips. Should we wet them with some water?"

"Later, honey," said the nurse. "We ain't got time right now."

CHAPTER EIGHTY-THREE

Ox and Barbara were sitting in the living room.

"I love this time of night," said Barbara. "It's like the calm after the storm."

"That's certainly better than the calm before the storm," said Ox.

"I guess the word 'storm' really describes the mess with all those nursing homes."

"Yes," said Ox, "and it's not over yet. There are still nursing homes out of compliance. The Nursing Home Watch Committee will be concentrating on homes in the southwest of Philadelphia for a few months."

"Some people will do anything to make money. Nursing homes that prey on the helpless are truly vultures. If only the roles could be reversed," said Barbara. "Speaking of vultures, which nursing home did the police say Bush is in?"

"Place called the Love Nest. Maybe someday our group will visit the place."

"Sounds like he's never going to be a threat to anybody again."

"Sounds like he's pretty much a vegetable."

"Well, he's earned whatever he's getting," said Barbara.

"Well, you know what they say, 'what goes around comes around.'"

"Sounds pretty dumb, but anyhow, justice is served."

"That's what they say."

Ox yawned, He felt relaxed. Things seemed to be moving in the right direction. "Rebecca is safe at our own facility now. One Soul House can hold up to forty patients. Maybe some of our other churches will start one, too."

Barbara shook her head. "I still can't get over that diamond business. It was kind of like a last assault. Steal their organs and then burn them for their ashes. There was an advertisement some while back to convert your loved one's ashes to a diamond as a keepsake. I could see that. In fact, it's a lovely idea. I've heard of people saving a lock of hair in a locket from a loved one. And there are lockets and lapel pins and vials for cremation ashes. So a ring, or tie tack cremation diamond or a cremation diamond pendant would be a perfect memorial."

"I'd rather hang around your neck before I'm cooked to a diamond."

"Well, you're just a diamond in the rough."

It was quiet. The children were in bed. There was a *thump thump* on the floor from the room above.

Ox smiled. "There goes Billy again. We might have to go up and tuck him in again."

"That's the third time," said Barbara. "After the fourth time, he usually gets tired enough to settle down and go to sleep."

"I wonder what goes through his mind with all the jumping each night."

"Do you remember what flitted through your mind when you were that age?" asked Barbara.

"A few things."

"Like what?"

"I disremember."

"Uh-huh."

After a while, a fourth series of thumps came. Then it got quiet.

ABOUT THE AUTHOR

William T. Delamar was born in Durham, North Carolina, in a home full of books, which ignited a love for reading. In high school, he worked part-time at Duke University Press, further increasing his insatiable desire for literature.

He served in the navy as a weatherman, received his bachelor's degree from the University of Pittsburgh, and a master's degree from Antioch University. After thirty-five years' experience in hospital organization and development, ranging from methods and procedures examiner to CEO, Delamar became a founding member of the Hospital Management and Information Society. Under his guidance, it grew from twenty-eight members to thousands internationally.

Delamar was on the board of the Philadelphia Writers' Conference, having served five times as president. His works include: *The Hidden Congregation*, *The Caretakers*, *Patients in Purgatory*, and *The Brother Voice*. He crossed over to join his wife Gloria in 2022.

THE REVEREND CHRISTIE MYSTERIES

FROM OPEN ROAD MEDIA

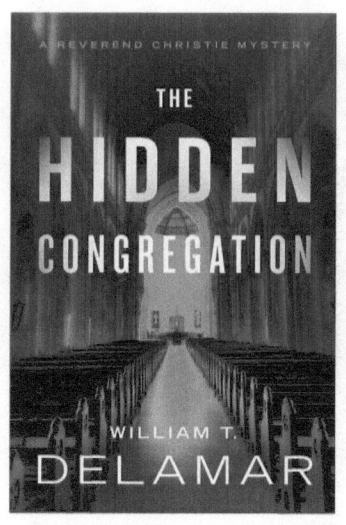

OPEN ROAD

INTEGRATED MEDIA

Find a full list of our authors and
titles at www.openroadmedia.com

FOLLOW US
@OpenRoadMedia